"*The Body Artist* is brief, oblique,
exquisitely tentative . . . DeLillo at his
understatedly dramatic best . . . This is a richly
gifted writer of fiction both doing it and at
the same time showing how it is done"
Dublin Irish Times

"Though the book is less than half the length
of *White Noise* and *Underworld*, it can more than
hold its own in their company. Its alternating
moods of terror and pity, humor and a certain
wistfulness, ensure that *The Body Artist*
will be hard to forget"
Washington Post

"Compelling, lucid and disturbing, this
short novel is a masterly portrayal of faltering
human relationships"
Marie Claire

"Compact, emotional and hard . . . This is an
unusual book about both heart and head, and the
way they sometimes get lost in one another"
The Times

THE BODY ARTIST

Don DeLillo is the acclaimed author
of fifteen novels and three plays. He has won
the National Book Award, the Jerusalem Prize, the
Irish Times International Fiction Prize and most
recently the PEN/Saul Bellow Award for lifetime
achivement in American literature.

ALSO BY DON DELILLO

THE BODY ARTIST

DON DELILLO

PICADOR

First published 2001 by Scribner, a division of Simon & Schuster, US, New York

First published in Great Britain 2001 by Picador

New edition published 2002 by Picador

This edition published 2011 by Picador
an imprint of Pan Macmillan, a division of Macmillan Publishers Limited
Pan Macmillan, 20 New Wharf Road, London N1 9RR
Basingstoke and Oxford
Associated companies throughout the world
www.panmacmillan.com

ISBN 978-0-330-52495-7

A CIP catalogue record for this book is available from
the British Library.

Typeset by SetSystems Ltd, Saffron Walden, Essex
Printed in the UK by CPI Mackays, Chatham ME8 5TD

Visit www.picador.com to read more about all our books
and to buy them. You will also find features, author interviews and
news of any author events, and you can sign up for e-newsletters
so that you're always first to hear about our new releases.

THE BODY ARTIST

1

Time seems to pass. The world happens, unrolling into moments, and you stop to glance at a spider pressed to its web. There is a quickness of light and a sense of things outlined precisely and streaks of running luster on the bay. You know more surely who you are on a strong bright day after a storm when the smallest falling leaf is stabbed with self-awareness. The wind makes a sound in the pines and the world comes into being, irreversibly, and the spider rides the wind-swayed web.

It happened this final morning that they were here at the same time, in the kitchen, and they shambled past each other to get things out of cabinets and drawers and then waited one for the other by the sink or fridge, still a little puddled in dream melt, and she ran tap water over the blueberries bunched in her hand and closed her eyes to breathe the savor rising.

He sat with the newspaper, stirring his coffee. It was his coffee and his cup. They shared the newspaper but it was actually, unspokenly, hers.

"I want to say something but what."

She ran water from the tap and seemed to notice. It was the first time she'd ever noticed this.

"About the house. This is what it is," he said. "Something I meant to tell you."

She noticed how water from the tap turned opaque in seconds. It ran silvery and clear and then in seconds turned opaque and how curious it seemed that in all these months and all these times in which she'd run water from the kitchen tap she'd never noticed how the water ran clear at first and then went not murky exactly but opaque, or maybe it hadn't happened before, or she'd noticed and forgotten.

She crossed to the cabinet with the blueberries wet in her hand and reached up for the cereal and took the box to the counter, the mostly brown and white box, and then the toaster thing popped and she flipped it down again because it took two flips to get the bread to go brown and he absently nodded his acknowledgment because it was his toast and his

4

butter and then he turned on the radio and got the weather.

The sparrows were at the feeder, wing-beating, fighting for space on the curved perches.

She reached into the near cabinet for a bowl and shook some cereal out of the box and then dropped the berries on top. She rubbed her hand dry on her jeans, feeling a sense somewhere of the color blue, runny and wan.

What's it called, the lever. She'd pressed down the lever to get his bread to go brown.

It was his toast, it was her weather. She listened to reports and called the weather number frequently and sometimes stood out front and looked into the coastal sky, tasting the breeze for latent implications.

"Yes exactly. I know what it is," he said.

She went to the fridge and opened the door. She stood there remembering something.

She said, "What?" Meaning what did you say, not what did you want to tell me.

She remembered the soya granules. She crossed to the cabinet and took down the box and then caught the fridge door before it swung shut. She reached in for the milk, realizing what it was he'd said that she hadn't heard about eight seconds ago.

Every time she had to bend and reach into the lower and remote parts of the refrigerator she let out a groan, but not really every time, that resembled a life lament. She was too trim and limber to feel the strain and was only echoing Rey, identifyingly, groaning his groan, but in a manner so seamless and deep it was her discomfort too.

Now that he'd remembered what he meant to tell her, he seemed to lose interest. She didn't have to see his face to know this. It was in the air. It was in the pause that trailed from his remark of eight, ten, twelve seconds ago. Something insignificant. He would take it as a kind of self-diminishment, bringing up a matter so trivial.

She went to the counter and poured soya over the cereal and fruit. The lever sprang or sprung and he got up and took his toast back to the table and then went for the butter and she had to lean away from the counter when he approached, her milk carton poised, so he could open the drawer and get a butter knife.

There were voices on the radio in like Hindi it sounded.

She poured milk into the bowl. He sat down and got up. He went to the fridge and got the orange juice and stood in the middle of the room shaking the carton to float the pulp and make the juice thicker. He never remembered the juice until the toast was done. Then he shook the carton. Then he poured the juice and watched a skim of sizzling foam appear at the top of the glass.

She picked a hair out of her mouth. She stood at the counter looking at it, a short pale strand that wasn't hers and wasn't his.

He stood shaking the container. He shook it longer than he had to because he wasn't paying attention, she thought, and because it was satisfying in some dumb and blameless way, for its own childlike sake, for the bounce and slosh and cardboard orange aroma.

He said, "Do you want some of this?"

She was looking at the hair.

"Tell me because I'm not sure. Do you drink juice?" he said, still shaking the damn thing, two fingers pincered at the spout.

She scraped her upper teeth over her tongue to rid her system of the complicated sense memory of someone else's hair.

She said, "What? Never drink the stuff. You know that. How long have we been living together?"

"Not long," he said.

He got a glass, poured the juice and watched the foam appear. Then he wheeled a little achingly into his chair.

"Not long enough for me to notice the details," he said.

"I always think this isn't supposed to happen here. I think anywhere but here."

He said, "What?"

"A hair in my mouth. From someone else's head."

He buttered his toast.

"Do you think it only happens in big cities with mixed populations?"

"Anywhere but here." She held the strand of hair between thumb and index finger, regarding it with mock aversion, or real aversion stretched to artistic limits, her mouth at a palsied slant. "That's what I think."

"Maybe you've been carrying it since childhood." He went back to the newspaper. "Did you have a pet dog?"

"Hey. What woke *you* up?" she said.

It was her newspaper. The telephone was his except when she was calling the weather. They both used the computer but it was spiritually hers.

She stood at the counter looking at the hair. Then she snapped it off her fingers to the floor. She turned to the sink and ran hot water over her hand and then took the cereal bowl to the table. Birds scattered when she moved near the window.

"I've seen you drink gallons of juice, tremendous, how can I tell you?" he said.

Her mouth was still twisted from the experience of sharing some food handler's unknown life or from a reality far stranger and more meandering, the intimate passage of the hair from person to person and somehow mouth to mouth across years and cities and diseases and unclean foods and many baneful body fluids.

"What? I don't think so," she said.

Okay, she put the bowl on the table. She went to the stove, got the kettle and filled it from the tap. He changed stations on the radio and said something she missed. She took the kettle back to the stove because this is how you live a life even if you don't know it and then she scraped her teeth over her tongue again, for emphasis, watching the flame shoot blue from the burner.

She'd had to sort of jackknife away from the counter when he approached to get the butter knife.

She moved toward the table and the birds went cracking off the feeder again. They passed out of the shade beneath the eaves and flew into sunglare and silence and it was an action she only partly saw, elusive and mutely beautiful, the birds so sunstruck they were consumed by light, disembodied, turned into something sheer and fleet and scatter-bright.

She sat down and picked through sections of newspaper and realized she had no spoon. She had no spoon. She looked at him and saw he was sporting a band-aid at the side of his jaw.

She used the old dented kettle instead of the new one she'd just bought because—she didn't know why. It was an old frame house that had many rooms and working fireplaces and animals in the walls and mildew everywhere, a place they'd rented unseen, a relic of the boom years of the lumbering and ship-building trades, way too big, and there were creaking floorboards and a number of bent utensils dating to god knows.

She half fell out of her chair in a gesture of self-ridicule and went to the counter to get a spoon. She took the soya granules back to the table as well. The soya had a smell that didn't seem to belong to the sandy stuff in the box. It was a faint wheaty stink with feet mixed in. Every time she used the soya she smelled it. She smelled it two or three times.

"Cut yourself again."

"What?" He put his hand to his jaw, head sunk in the newspaper. "Just a nick."

She started to read a story in her part of the

paper. It was an old newspaper, Sunday's, from town, because there were no deliveries here.

"That's lately, I don't know, maybe you shouldn't shave first thing. Wake up first. Why shave at all? Let your mustache grow back. Grow a beard."

"Why shave at all? There must be a reason," he said. "I want God to see my face."

He looked up from the paper and laughed in the empty way she didn't like. She took a bite of cereal and looked at another story. She tended lately to place herself, to insert herself into certain stories in the newspaper. Some kind of daydream variation. She did it and then became aware she was doing it and then sometimes did it again a few minutes later with the same or a different story and then became aware again.

She reached for the soya box without looking up from the paper and poured some granules into the bowl and the radio played traffic and talk.

The idea seemed to be that she'd have to wear out the old kettle, use it and use it until it developed rust bubbles and then and only then would it be okay for her to switch to the kettle she'd just bought.

"Do you have to listen to the radio?"

"No," she said and read the paper. "What?"

"It is such astonishing shit."

The way he stressed the *t* in shit, dignifying the word.

"I didn't turn on the radio. You turned on the radio," she said.

He went to the fridge and came back with a large dark fig and turned off the radio.

"Give me some of that," she said, reading the paper.

"I was not blaming. Who turned it on, who turned it off. Someone's a little edgy this morning. I'm the one, what do I say, who should be defensive. Not the young woman who eats and sleeps and lives forever."

"What? Hey, Rey. Shut up."

He bit off the stem and tossed it toward the sink. Then he split the fig open with his thumbnails and took the spoon out of her hand and licked it off and used it to scoop a measure of claret flesh out of the gaping fig skin. He dropped this stuff on his toast—the flesh, the mash, the pulp—and then spread it with the bottom of the spoon, blood-buttery swirls that popped with seedlife.

"I'm the one to be touchy in the morning. I'm the one to moan. The terror of another ordinary day," he said slyly. "You don't know this yet."

"Give us all a break," she told him.

She leaned forward, he extended the bread. There were crows in the trees near the house, taking up a raucous call. She took a bite and closed her eyes so she could think about the taste.

He gave back her spoon. Then he turned on the radio and remembered he'd just turned it off and he turned it off again.

She poured granules into the bowl. The smell of the soya was somewhere between body odor, yes, in the lower extremities and some authentic pod-life of the earth, deep and seeded. But that didn't describe it. She read a story in the paper about a child abandoned in some godforsaken. Nothing described it. It was pure smell. It was the thing that smell is, apart from all sources. It was as though and she nearly said something to this effect because it might amuse him but then she let it drop—it was as though some, maybe, medieval scholastic had attempted to classify all known odors and had found something that did not fit into his system and had called it soya, which could easily be part of a lofty Latin term, but no it couldn't, and she sat thinking of something, she wasn't sure what, with the spoon an inch from her mouth.

He said, "What?"

"I didn't say anything."

She got up to get something. She looked at the kettle and realized that wasn't it. She knew it would come to her because it always did and then it did.

She wanted honey for her tea even though the water wasn't boiling yet. She had a hyper-preparedness, or haywire, or hair-trigger, and Rey was always saying, or said once, and she carried a voice in her head that was hers and it was dialogue or monologue and she went to the cabinet where she got the honey and the tea bags—a voice that flowed from a story in the paper.

"Weren't you going to tell me something?"

He said, "What?"

She put a hand on his shoulder and moved past to her side of the table. The birds broke off the feeder in a wing-whir that was all *b*'s and *r*'s, the letter *b* followed by a series of vibrato *r*'s. But that wasn't it at all. That wasn't anything like it.

"You said something. I don't know. The house."

"It's not interesting. Forget it."

"I don't want to forget it."

"It's not interesting. Let me put it another way. It's boring."

"Tell me anyway."

"It's too early. It's an effort. It's boring."

"You're sitting there talking. Tell me," she said.

She took a bite of cereal and read the paper.

"It's an effort. It's like what. It's like pushing a boulder."

"You're sitting there talking."

"Here," he said.

"You said the house. Nothing about the house is boring. I like the house."

"You like everything. You love everything. You're my happy home. Here," he said.

He handed her what remained of his toast and she chewed it mingled with cereal and berries. Suddenly she knew what he'd meant to tell her. She heard the crows in large numbers now, clamorous in the trees, probably mobbing a hawk.

"Just tell me. Takes only a second," she said, knowing absolutely what it was.

She saw him move his hand to his breast pocket and then pause and lower it to the cup. It was his coffee, his cup and his cigarette. How an incident described in the paper seemed to rise out of the inky lines of print and gather her into it. You separate the Sunday sections.

"Just tell me okay. Because I know anyway."

He said, "What? You insist you will drag this thing out of me. Lucky we don't normally have breakfast together. Because my mornings."

"I know anyway. So tell me."

He was looking at the paper.

"You know. Then fine. I don't have to tell you."

He was reading, getting ready to go for his cigarettes.

15

She said, "The noise."

He looked at her. He looked. Then he gave her the great smile, the gold teeth in the great olive-dark face. She hadn't seen this in a while, the amplified smile, Rey emergent, his eyes clear and lit, deep lines etched about his mouth.

"The noises in the walls. Yes. You've read my mind."

"It was one noise. It was one noise," she said. "And it wasn't in the walls."

"One noise. Okay. I haven't heard it lately. This is what I wanted to say. It's gone. Finished. End of conversation."

"True. Except I heard it yesterday, I think."

"Then it's not gone. Good. I'm happy for you."

"It's an old house. There's always a noise. But this is different. Not those damn scampering animals we hear at night. Or the house settling. I don't know," she said, not wanting to sound concerned. "Like there's something."

She read the paper, voice trailing off.

"Good. I'm glad," he said. "You need the company."

You separate the Sunday sections and there are endless identical lines of print with people living somewhere in the words and the strange contained reality of paper and ink seeps through the house for

16

a week and when you look at a page and distinguish one line from another it begins to gather you into it and there are people being tortured halfway around the world, who speak another language, and you have conversations with them more or less uncontrollably until you become aware you are doing it and then you stop, seeing whatever is in front of you at the time, like half a glass of juice in your husband's hand.

She took a bite of cereal and forgot to taste it. She lost the taste somewhere between the time she put the food in her mouth and the regretful second she swallowed it.

He put down the juice glass. He took the pack out of his shirt and lit up a cigarette, the cigarette he'd been smoking with his coffee since he was twelve years old, he'd told her, and he let the match burn down a bit before he shook it out in meditative slow motion and put it at the edge of his plate. It was agreeable to her, the smell of tobacco. It was part of her knowledge of his body. It was the aura of the man, a residue of smoke and unbroken habit, a dimension in the night, and she lapped it off the curled gray hairs on his chest and tasted it in his mouth. It was who he was in the dark, cigarettes and mumbled sleep and a hundred other things nameable and not.

But it wasn't one of his, the hair she'd found in her mouth. Employees must wash hands before leaving toilet. It was his toast but she'd eaten nearly half of it. It was his coffee and cup. Touch his cup and he looks at you edgewise, with the formal one-eyed glare of a boxer touching gloves. But she knew she was making this up because he didn't give a damn what you did with his cup. There were plenty of cups he could use. The phone was his. The birds were hers, the sparrows pecking at sunflower seeds. The hair was somebody else's.

He said something about his car, the mileage, gesturing. He liked to conduct, to guide an extended remark with his hand, a couple of fingers jutting.

"All day yesterday I thought it was Friday."

He said, "What?"

Or you become someone else, one of the people in the story, doing dialogue of your own devising. You become a man at times, living between the lines, doing another version of the story.

She thought and read. She groped for the soya box and her hand struck the juice container. She looked up and understood he wasn't reading the paper. He was looking at it but not reading it and she understood this retroactively, that he'd been looking at it all this time but not absorbing the words on the page.

18

The container remained upright. She poured a little more soya into the bowl, for grainy texture and long life.

"All day yesterday I thought it was Friday."

He said, "Was it?"

She remembered to smile.

He said, "What does it matter anyway?"

She'd put a hand on his shoulder and then nearly moved it up along the back of his neck and into his hair, caressingly, but hadn't.

"I'm only saying. How does it happen that Thursday seems like Friday? We're out of the city. We're off the calendar. Friday shouldn't have an identity here. Who wants more coffee?"

She went to pour water for her tea and paused at the stove, waiting for him to say yes or no to coffee. When she started back she saw a blue jay perched atop the feeder. She stopped dead and held her breath. It stood large and polished and looked royally remote from the other birds busy feeding and she could nearly believe she'd never seen a jay before. It stood enormous, looking in at her, seeing whatever it saw, and she wanted to tell Rey to look up.

She watched it, black-barred across the wings and tail, and she thought she'd somehow only now learned how to look. She'd never seen a thing so clearly and it was not simply because the jay was posted where it was, close enough for her to note the details of cresting and color. There was also the clean shock of its appearance among the smaller brownish birds, its mineral blue and muted blue and broad dark neckband. But if Rey looked up, the bird would fly.

She tried to work past the details to the bird itself, nest thief and skilled mimic, to the fixed interest in those eyes, a kind of inquisitive chill that felt a little like a challenge.

When birds look into houses, what impossible worlds they see. Think. What a shedding of every knowable surface and process. She wanted to believe the bird was seeing her, a woman with a teacup in her hand, and never mind the folding back of day and night, the apparition of a space set off from time. She looked and took a careful breath. She was alert to the clarity of the moment but knew it was ending already. She felt it in the blue jay. Or maybe not. She was making it happen herself because she could not look any longer. This must be what it means to see if you've been near blind all your life. She said something to Rey, who lifted his head slightly, chasing the jay but leaving the sparrows unstartled.

"Did you see it?"

He half turned to answer.

"Don't we see them all the time?"

"Not all the time. And never so close."

"Never so close. Okay."

"It was looking at me."

"It was looking at you."

She was standing in place, off his left shoulder. When she moved toward her chair the sparrows flew.

"It was watching me."

"Did it make your day?"

"It made my day. My week. What else?"

She drank her tea and read. Nearly everything she read sent her into reverie.

She turned on the radio and tracked slowly along the dial, reading the paper, trying to find the weather on the radio.

He finished his coffee and smoked.

She sat over the bowl of cereal. She looked past the bowl into a space inside her head that was also here in front of her.

She folded a section of newspaper and read a line or two and read some more or didn't, sipping tea and drifting.

The radio reported news about a missile exploding mysteriously, underground, in Montana, and she didn't catch if it was armed or not.

He smoked and looked out the window to his right, where an untended meadow tumbled to the rutted dirt road that led to a gravel road.

She read and drifted. She was here and there.

The tea had no honey in it. She'd left the honey jar unopened by the stove.

He looked around for an ashtray.

She had a conversation with a doctor in a news story.

There were two miles of gravel before you reached the paved road that led to town.

She took the fig off his plate and put a finger down into it and reamed around inside for flesh.

A voice reported the weather but she missed it. She didn't know it was the weather until it was gone.

He eased his head well back and rolled it slowly side to side to lessen the tension in his neck.

She sucked the finger on her fig-dipping hand and thought of things they needed from the store.

He turned off the radio.

She sipped her tea and read. She more or less saw herself talking to a doctor in the bush somewhere, with people hungry in the dust.

The cigarette was burning down in his hand.

She picked up the soya box and tipped it toward her face and smelled inside.

When he walked out of the room, she realized there was something she wanted to tell him.

Sometimes she doesn't think of what she wants to say to him until he walks out of whatever room they're in. Then she thinks of it. Then she either calls after him or doesn't and he responds or doesn't.

She sat there and finished her tea and thought of what she thought of, memory traces and flary images and a friend she missed and all the shadow-dappled stuff of an undividable moment on a normal morning going crazy in ways so humanly routine you can't even stop and take note except for the Ajax she needs to buy and the birds behind her, rattling the metal frame of the feeder.

It's such a stupid thing to do, read the newspaper and eat.

She saw him standing in the doorway.

"Have you seen my keys?"

She said, "What?"

He waited for the question to register.

"Which keys?" she said.

He looked at her.

She said, "I bought some lotion yesterday. Which I meant to tell you. It's a muscle rub. It's in a green and white tube on the shelf in the big bathroom upstairs. It's greaseless. It's a muscle rub. Rub it in, my love. Or ask me nice, I'll do it for you."

"All my keys are on one ring," he said.

She almost said, Is that smart? But then she didn't. Because what a needless thing. Because how petty it would be to say such a thing, in the morning or any time, on a strong bright day after a storm.

REY ROBLES, 64,
CINEMA'S POET OF LONELY PLACES

Rey Robles, who directed two world-renowned movies of the late 1970s, was found dead Sunday morning in the Manhattan apartment of his first wife, the fashion consultant Isabel Corrales.

The cause of death was a self-inflicted gunshot wound, according to police who were called to the scene.

Mr. Robles's accounts of his early life were inconsistent but the most persuasive independent versions suggest he was 64 at his death.

He was born Alejandro Alquezar, in Barcelona. A biographical sketch in the journal *Cahiers du Cinéma* asserted that his father, a worker in a textile plant and a militant antifascist, was killed in that city during the fiercest street fighting of the civil war. The article cites evidence that Alejandro, still a small boy, was among the "war children" of Spain who were sent to the Soviet Union by their families when the dictatorship of the right became an impending reality.

It isn't clear how many years he spent in the USSR or whether he was ever reunited with his mother. It is known that he lived in Paris as a young man, hauling trash, performing as a street juggler and playing bit parts in several movies, cast as a thief or pimp. This is when he adopted the name Rey Robles, after a minor character he played in an obscure film noir.

He spent a few years in New York writing subtitles for a trickle of Spanish-language and Russian films and then went west, finding work as a uniformed chauffeur in Los Angeles, where he continued a fringe relationship with the movies, appearing as an extra in half a dozen films. He got a start on the other side of the camera after he became the personal driver of a multimillionaire cement manufacturer from Liechtenstein, a man who was a heavy investor in international film projects. By his own account, Mr. Robles had an affair with the man's wife and persuaded her to arrange a job for him as a second-unit director on a spaghetti western scheduled to be shot in Spain.

Ten years later, at the Cannes Film Festival, Mr. Robles told an appreciative audience, "The answer to life is the movies."

He directed eight features in all. The third of these, *My Life for Yours*, a French-Italian co-production about a wealthy woman kidnapped by Corsican bandits, won the Palme d'Or at Cannes. It was followed by *Polaris*, a tense American crime drama with an undercurrent of Spanish surrealism. The film developed a cult following and ran for extended periods in a number of art houses in this country and abroad.

"His work at its best extends the language of film," wrote the critic Philip Stansky. "His subject is people in landscapes of estrangement. He found a spiritual knife-edge in the poetry of alien places, where extreme situations become inevitable and characters are forced toward life-defining moments."

His subsequent movies failed commercially and were largely dismissed by critics. Friends of Mr. Robles attribute his decline to alcoholism and intermittent depression. He married the stage actress Anna Langdon during this period. They separated shortly afterward amid lurid headlines in the British tabloids and were eventually divorced.

He is survived by his third wife, Lauren Hartke, the body artist.

2

It's a hazy white day and the highway lifts to a drained sky. There are four northbound lanes and you are driving in the third lane and there are cars ahead and behind and to both sides, although not too many and not too close. When you reach the top of the incline, something happens and the cars begin to move unhurriedly now, seemingly self-propelled, coasting smoothly on the level surface. Everything is slow and hazy and drained and it all happens around the word *seem*. All the cars including yours seem to flow in dissociated motion, giving the impression of or presenting the appearance of, and the highway runs in a white hum.

Then the mood passes. The noise and rush and blur are back and you slide into your life again, feeling the painful weight in your chest.

*

She thought of these days as the first days back.

In the first days back she restocked the pantry and sprayed chemicals on the bathroom tile. There was a full-size pantry, a dark musty room off the kitchen, and it didn't need restocking. She cleaned and filled the bird feeders, shaping the day around a major thing with all its wrinkles and twists, its array of swarming variations. She sprayed the tile and porcelain with pine-scent chemicals, half addicted to the fumes. There were two months left on the rental agreement. They'd rented for six and now there were two. One person, two months. She used a bottle with a pistol-grip attachment.

It felt like home, being here, and she raced through the days with their small ravishing routines, days the same, paced and organized but with a simultaneous wallow, uncentered, sometimes blank in places, days that moved so slow they ached.

She looked at the pages she'd been working on with Rey, his bullshit autobiography. The hard copy sat there, stark against her sense of his spoken recollections, the tapestried lies and contrivances, stories shaped out of desperations not always clear to her. She hand-patted through the clothes he'd left in the bedroom closet. She was not undone by the things that people leave behind when they die and she put the clothes in a box for the needy.

When she was downstairs she felt him in the rooms on the second floor. He used to prowl these rooms talking into a tiny tape recorder, smoke in his face, reciting ideas about some weary script to a writer somewhere whose name he could never recall. Now he was the smoke, Rey was, the thing in the air, vaporous, drifting into every space sooner or later, unshaped, but with a face that was somehow part of the presence, specific to the prowling man.

She climbed the stairs, hearing the sound a person makes who is climbing stairs, and she touched the oak grain of the newel when she reached the landing.

It was okay. She wanted to be here and she'd be okay. All their marriage, all the time they'd lived together they'd lived right here.

Her body felt different to her in ways she did not understand. Tight, framed, she didn't know exactly. Slightly foreign and unfamiliar. Different, thinner, didn't matter.

There was a package of bread crumbs on one of the shelves in the pantry. She knew she'd seen wax paper somewhere in a blue and something box. These were the things that were important now. Meals, tasks, errands.

She stepped slowly through the rooms. She felt him behind her when she was getting undressed, standing barefoot on the cold floor, throwing off a grubby sweater, and she half turned toward the bed.

In the first days back she got out of the car once and nearly collapsed—not the major breakdown of every significant function but a small helpless sinking toward the ground, a kind of forgetting how to stand.

She thought about broiling a cutlet, self-consciously alone, more or less seeing herself from the edge of the room or standing precisely where she was and being who she was and seeing a smaller hovering her in the air somewhere, already thinking it's tomorrow.

She wanted to disappear in Rey's smoke, be dead, be him, and she tore the wax paper along the serrated edge of the box and reached for the carton of bread crumbs.

When the phone rang she did not look at it the way they do in the movies. Real people don't look at ringing phones.

The wax paper separated from the roll in rat-a-tat sequence, advancing along the notched edge of the box, and she heard it along her spine, she thought.

She was always thinking into tomorrow. She

planned the days in advance. She sat in the panelled room. She stood in the tub and sprayed high on the tile walls until the depraved pine reek of acid and ether began to overwhelm her. It was hard to stop pressing the trigger.

She burned her hand on the skillet and went right to the fridge and there was no ice in the fucking. She hadn't filled the fucking ice thing.

People pick up ringing phones or don't. She listened to it ring. It sounded through the house, all the handsets jingling in their cradles.

How completely strange it suddenly seemed that major corporations mass-produced bread crumbs and packaged and sold them everywhere in the world and she looked at the bread-crumb carton for the first true time, really seeing it and understanding what was in it, and it was bread crumbs.

She sat in the panelled room and tried to read. First she'd build a fire. It was a room designed aspiringly for a brandy and a fire, a failed room, perversely furnished, and she drank tea and tried to read a book. But she'd make her way through a page and stare indifferently at objects fixed in space.

In the first days back she ate a clam from hell and spent a number of subsequent hours scuttling to the toilet. But at least she had her body back. There's nothing like a raging crap, she thought, to make mind and body one.

She climbed the stairs, hearing herself from other parts of the house somehow.

She threw off a grubby sweater. She raised her arm out of the sweater and struck her hand lightly on something above, wondering what it was, although this had happened before, and then she remembered the hanging lamp, metal shade wobbling, the lamp that was totally wrong for the room, and she turned toward the bed and looked, half looked, not looked in expectation but something else—a meaning so thin she could not read it.

There were too many things to understand and finally just one.

In town she saw a white-haired woman, Japanese, alone on a stone path in front of her house. She held a garden hose and stood weightless under lowering skies, so flat and still she might be gift wrap, and she watered a border of scarlet phlox, a soft spray arching from the nozzle.

Things she saw seemed doubtful—not doubtful but ever changing, plunged into metamorphosis, something that is also something else, but what, and what.

She began to pick up the phone. She used a soft voice at first, not quite her own, a twisted tentative other's voice, to say hello, who is this, yes. Word had gotten around that she was here and the calls were from New York, where she lived, and from friends and colleagues in other cities. They called from the cities to tell her they didn't understand why she'd come back here. It was the last place she ought to be, alone in a large house on an empty coast, and she stepped through the rooms and climbed the stairs and planned the days in advance because there was more to do in less time as the light grew threatened. You looked and it was dark, always unexpected.

She woke early every morning and this was the worst time, the first murderous instant of lying in bed and remembering something and knowing in the flow of the same breath what it was.

They called five or six times a day and then a little less and she thought of the Japanese woman, a beautiful and problematic thing, if she is Japanese at all, watering her garden when the sky shows rain.

She took the tin-can ferry to Little Moon, where there was nothing to do but walk along a muddy path to the other end of the island past wind-beaten houses and a church with a missing steeple, a forty-minute march to an abandoned crafts center, quilting and woodcarving maybe and pottery by all means, and then briskly back again. The ferry ran on a schedule and this was reason enough to make the trip now and then.

The plan was to organize time until she could live again.

After the first days back she began to do her breathing exercises. There was bodywork to resume, her regimen of cat stretch and methodical contortion. She worked from the spine outward, moving along the floor on all fours, and she felt her aorta recoil to every blood surge. There were headstands and neck-rolls. She stuck out her tongue and panted in tightly timed sequence, internally timed, an exactitude she knew in the bones that were separated by the disks that went rat-a-tat down her back.

But the world was lost inside her.

At night the sky was very near, sprawled in star smoke and gamma cataclysms, but she didn't see it the way she used to, as soul extension, dumb guttural wonder, a thing that lived outside language in the oldest part of her.

She stopped listening to weather reports. She took the weather as it came, chill rain and blowy days and the great hunched boulders in the slant fields, like clan emblems, pulsing with stormlight and story and time. She chopped firewood. She spent hours at the computer screen looking at a live-streaming video feed from the edge of a two-lane road in a city in Finland. It was the middle of the night in Kotka, in Finland, and she watched the screen. It was interesting to her because it was happening now, as she sat here, and because it happened twenty-four hours a day, facelessly, cars entering and leaving Kotka, or just the empty road in the dead times. The dead times were best.

She sat and looked at the screen. It was compelling to her, real enough to withstand the circumstance of nothing going on. It thrived on the circumstance. It was three in the morning in Kotka and she waited for a car to come along—not that she wondered who was in it. It was simply the fact of Kotka. It was the sense of organization, a place contained in an unyielding frame, as it is and as you watch, with a reading of local time in the digital display in a corner of the screen. Kotka was another world but she could see it in its realness, in its hours, minutes and seconds.

She imagined that someone might masturbate to this, the appearance of a car on the road to Kotka in the middle of the night. It made her want to laugh. She chopped firewood. She set aside time every day for the webcam at Kotka. She didn't know the meaning of this feed but took it as an act of floating poetry. It was best in the dead times. It emptied her mind and made her feel the deep silence of other places, the mystery of seeing over the world to a place stripped of everything but a road that approaches and recedes, both realities occurring at once, and the numbers changed in the digital display with an odd and hollow urgency, the seconds advancing toward the minute, the minutes climbing hourward, and she sat and watched, waiting for a car to take fleeting shape on the roadway.

Mariella called, her friend, a writer in New York.

"Are you all right?"

"What am I supposed to say?"

"I don't know. But are you lonely?"

"There ought to be another word for it. Everyone's lonely. This is something else."

"But don't you think. I don't know. It would be easier."

"This is the kind of conversation you ought to have with someone else. I don't know how to have these conversations."

"If you didn't separate yourself. You need to

be around familiar people and things. Alone is no good. I know how you felt about him. And how devastating. God. But you don't want to fold up into yourself. I also know you're determined. You're strong-willed in your creepy-crawly way. But you have to direct yourself out of this thing, not into it. Don't fold up."

"Tell me what you're doing."

"Feeding my face. Looking out the window," Mariella said. "Talking to you."

"What are you eating?"

"Carrot sticks."

"This is not feeding your face."

"This is starving my body. I know. They're showing some of his early work at the Film Forum. You didn't know him that long. This could be a plus."

In the morning she heard the noise. It had the same sort of distinctness she'd noted the first time, about three months ago, when she and Rey had gone upstairs to investigate. He said it was a squirrel or raccoon trapped somewhere. She thought it was a calculated stealth. It had a certain measured quality. She didn't think it was an animal noise. It carried an effect that was nearly intimate, like something's here and breathing the same air we breathe and it moves the way we move. The noise had this quality, of a body shedding space, but there was no one there when they looked.

She was in the kitchen when she heard it this time. She carried her tea upstairs. The rooms at the end of the second-story hall. The dim third story, bulbs blown and most of the furniture removed. The short stairway to the cupola. She looked into the stillness, head swiveling, her upper body projected into the structure, which was fairly broad and used as storage space. Her tea was cold by the time she stood on the floor of the cupola. She poked into old clothing layered in cardboard boxes and looked at documents gone brittle in leather folders. There was a stuffed owl and a stack of unframed watercolors, badly warped. She saw a twirling leaf just outside the window. It was a small amber leaf twirling in the air beneath a tree branch that extended over the roof. There was no sign of a larva web from which the leaf might be suspended, or a strand of some bird's nest-building material. Just the leaf in midair, turning.

She found him the next day in a small bedroom off the large empty room at the far end of the hall on the third floor. He was smallish and fine-bodied and at first she thought he was a kid, sandy-haired and roused from deep sleep, or medicated maybe.

He sat on the edge of the bed in his underwear. In the first seconds she thought he was inevitable. She felt her way back in time to the earlier indications that there was someone in the house and she arrived at this instant, unerringly, with her perceptions all sorted and endorsed.

3

She looked at him.

"Tell me. You've been here how long?"

He didn't raise his head. There was something so strange about him that she heard her words hang in the room, predictable and trite. She felt no fear. He had a foundling quality—lost and found—and she was, she guessed, the finder.

"You have been here," she said, speaking clearly, pausing between words.

He looked at her and seemed older now, the scant act of head-raising, a simple tilt of chin and eyes that was minutely crucial to his transformation—older and faintly moist, a sheen across his forehead and cheeks.

He said something.

She said, "What?"

His underwear consisted of white trunks and a

T-shirt that was too big and she studied him up and down, openly, everywhere.

"It is not able," he said.

"But why are you here? And have you been here for long?"

He dropped his head and appeared to think about these matters as if working out the details of a complicated problem.

They stood outside the house near the top of the sloped field and watched a lobsterboat pumping through the whitecaps. She'd fed him leftover soup and some bread, some toast. You had to flip the thing twice to get the bread to toast properly.

"What do you see?" she said, gesturing toward the boat and the advancing cloudline.

"The trees are some of them," he said.

"Bending. Swaying in the wind. Those are birches. The white ones. Those are called paper birches."

"The white ones."

"The white ones. But beyond the trees."

"Beyond the trees."

"Out there," she said.

He looked a while.

"It rained very much."

"It will rain. It is going to rain," she said.

He wore a windbreaker and a pair of workpants and seemed unhappy out here. She tried not to press him for information. She found the distance interesting, the halting quality of his speech and actions, the self-taught quality, his seeming unconcern about what would happen to him now. Not apathy or indifference, she thought, but his limited ability to consider the implications. She wasn't sure what it meant to him, being found in someone else's house.

The wind came harder now and they turned away from it. She amused herself by thinking he'd come from cyberspace, a man who'd emerged from her computer screen in the dead of night. He was from Kotka, in Finland.

She said, "It did not rain. It *will* rain."

He moved uneasily in space, indoors or out, as if the air had bends and warps. She watched him sidle into the house, walking with a slight shuffle. He feared levitation maybe. She could not stop watching him.

It was always as if. He did this or that as if. She needed a reference elsewhere to get him placed.

They sat in the grim panelled room under prints of sailing ships. The phone was ringing. He looked at the charred logs collapsed in the fireplace, last night's fire, and she watched him. The books on the low shelves were mostly summer reading you find in rented houses, books suited to the role, with faded jacket illustrations of other houses in other summers, or almanacs, or atlases, a sun stripe edging the tops of the taller books.

His chin was sunken back, severely receded, giving his face an unfinished look, and his hair was wiry and snagged, with jutting clumps.

She had to concentrate to note these features. She looked at him and had to look again. There was something elusive in his aspect, moment to moment, a thinness of physical address.

She whispered, "Talk to me."

He sat with his legs awkwardly crossed, one trouser leg riding up his calf, and she could see that he'd knotted a length of string around the top of his sock to keep it from sagging. It made her think of someone.

"Talk to me. I am talking," he said.

She thought she understood what he meant by this. There was a certain futility in his tone, an endlessness of effort, suggesting things he could not easily make clear to her no matter how much he said. Even his gestures seemed marked by struggle. She knew she would have to call hospitals and clinics, psychiatric facilities, to ask about a missing patient.

The rain hit the windows in taps and spatters, small and countable, and then it was everywhere, banging the roof of the sunporch and filling the downspouts, and they sat and listened to it.

She said, "What's your name?"

He looked at her.

She said, "I came here to be by myself. This is important to me. I am willing to wait. I will give you a chance to tell me who you are. But I don't want someone in my house. I will give you a chance," she said. "But I will not wait indefinitely."

She didn't want it to sound like a formal warning but it probably did. She would have to call the nearest mission for the homeless, which wouldn't be near at all, and maybe the church in town or the church with the missing steeple on Little Moon and she would have to call the police, finally, if nothing else worked.

"I am here because of Rey, who was my husband, who is dead. I don't know why I'm telling you this because it is surely unnecessary. But I need to live here alone for a time. Just tell me if you understand."

He moved his hand in a manner that seemed to mean she didn't have to say anything further. Of course he understood. But maybe not.

The storm rolled in and they sat and listened.

The rain was so total they had to listen to it. She could call the real estate agent and make a complaint about a person on the premises. That was another thing she could do.

It was only midmorning but she had the feeling he'd been here a week. They sat and looked at last night's fire.

Then she realized who it was, the man he made her think of.

It was a science teacher in high school, semi-bumbling, who looked pale-haired in uncertain light and bald on brighter days and who scotch-taped a split seam in his loafers once and spoke in unmeasured hesitations that made the students feel embarrassed on his behalf, the few sensitive ones, or openly restless, the restless, which was everybody else.

She named the visitor in his honor. Mr. Tuttle. She thought it would make him easier to see.

She whispered, "Tell me something."

He uncrossed his legs and sat with a hand on each knee, a dummy in a red club chair, his head turned toward her.

"I know how much." He said, "I know how much this house. Alone by the sea."

He looked not pleased exactly but otherwise satisfied, technically satisfied to have managed the last cluster of words. And it was in fact, coming from Mr. Tuttle, a formulation she heard in its echoing depths. Four words only. But he'd placed her in a set of counter-surroundings, of simultaneous insides and outsides. The house, the sea-planet outside it, and how the word *alone* referred to her and to the house and how the word *sea* reinforced the idea of solitude but suggested a vigorous release as well, a means of escape from the book-walled limits of the self.

She knew it was foolish to examine so closely. She was making things up. But this was the effect he had, shadow-inching through a sentence, showing a word in its facets and aspects, words like moons in particular phases.

She said, "I like the house. Yes, I want to be here. But it's only a rental. I am renting. I will be out of here in six or seven weeks. Less maybe. It's a house we rented. Five or six weeks. Less," she said.

She wasn't watching him now. She was looking at the backs of her hands, fingers stretched, looking and thinking, recalling moments with Rey, not moments exactly but times, or moments flowing into composite time, an erotic of see and touch, and she curled one hand over and into the other, missing him in her body and feeling sexually and abysmally alone and staring at the points where her knuckles shone bloodless from the pressure of her grip.

He said, "But you did not leave."

She looked at him.

"I will leave. In a few weeks. When it's time," she said. "When the lease is up. Or earlier. I will leave."

"But you do not," he said.

This shift from past tense to present had the sound of something overcome, an obstacle or restriction. He had to extend himself to get it out. And she heard something in his voice. She didn't know what it was but it made her get up and go to the window.

She stood there looking at the rain. She thought he might belong in one of the trailer homes scattered at the edge of the woods outside town, near but wholly remote, with cars on blocks and a wacko dog convoluted in the dirt and leaves, trying to scratch an itch somewhere, and he is the grown son who has always been this way, inaccessible, ever dependent, living matter-of-fact in an oblong box with his drained and aging parents, who never use each other's name, and he wanders off for days sometimes and goes wherever he goes, muttering and unharmed, into the bubble world.

Maybe not, she thought. That's not what she'd heard in his voice. There was something at the edge, unconnected to income levels or verb tenses or what his parents watch on TV.

She turned from the window and got him to talk a little. He seemed agreeable to the idea of talking. He talked about objects in the room, stumblingly, and she wondered what he saw, or failed to see, or saw so differently she could never begin to conjure its outlines.

He talked. After a while she began to understand what she was hearing. It took many levels of perception. It took whole social histories of how people listen to what other people say. There was a peculiarity in his voice, a trait developing even as he spoke, that she was able to follow to its source.

She watched him. He was the same hapless man she'd come upon earlier, without a visible sense of the effect he was having.

It wasn't outright impersonation but she heard elements of her voice, the clipped delivery, the slight buzz deep in the throat, her pitch, her sound, and how difficult at first, unearthly almost, to detect her own voice coming from someone else, from him, and then how deeply disturbing.

She wasn't sure it was her voice. Then she was.

By this time he wasn't talking about chairs, lamps or patterns in the carpet. He seemed to be assuming her part in a conversation with someone.

She tried to understand what she was hearing.

He gestured as he spoke, moving his hand to the words, and she began to realize she'd said these things to Rey, here in the house, or things similar. They were routine remarks about a call she'd had from friends who wanted to visit. She remembered, she recalled dimly that she'd been standing at the foot of the stairs and that he'd been on the second floor, Rey had, walking up and down the hall, doing scriptwork.

She stood by the window now. The voice began to waver and fade but his hand remained in motion, marking the feeble beat.

She grabbed a coat from the rack and went out in the rain. She draped the coat over her bent arm, which she held above her, and walked across the grass to the dirt driveway, where the car was parked. The door was unlocked and she got in and sat there because why would you lock the door in a place so isolated. Rain washed down the windshield in overlapping tides. She sat there in a brief fit of shivering and it was hard to stop hearing the sound of that voice. One of the rear windows was lowered an inch and the smell of wet meadow, the fragrance of country rain, the effects of sea and breeze and memory all mixed in the air but she kept hearing the voice and seeing the hand gesture, unmistakably Rey's, two fingers joined and wagging.

She didn't know how long she was there. Maybe a long time. The rain beat hard on the roof and hood. How much time is a long time? Could be this, could be that. Finally she pushed open the door and walked back to the house, holding the coat aloft.

4

There were five birds on the feeder and they all faced outward, away from the food and identically still. She watched them. They weren't looking or listening so much as feeling something, intent and sensing.

All these words are wrong, she thought.

This was the feeder that hung outside the sunporch and she stood in the mostly white room, by the broad window, waiting for Mr. Tuttle.

She'd been putting up feeders since her return. This was the basic range of her worldly surround, the breadth of nature that bordered the house. But it feels like she's feeding the birds of Earth, a different seed for each receptacle, sometimes two seeds layered light and dark in a single feeder, and they come and peck, or don't, and the feeders are different as well, cages, ringed cylinders, hanging saucers, mounted trays, and maybe it's a hawk, she doesn't know, that keeps the birds away sometimes, or a jay that mimics a hawk, or they read a message in some event outside the visible spectrum.

When he walked in he didn't look at her but went straight to the glass-top table with the curlicued legs.

Rey's tape recorder lay blinking in the middle of the table.

She sat and began to speak, describing his appearance. Face and hair and so forth. Wakeful or not. Fairly neat or mostly unkempt. What else? Good, bad or indifferent night.

Not that she knew what his nights were like. One night only. She hadn't been able to sleep and had stood for a while at his door past midnight, listening to the raspy nasal intake and finding herself moved in an unusual way. In sleep he was no more unknowable than anyone else. Look. The shrouded body feebly beating. This is what you feel, looking at the hushed and vulnerable body, almost anyone's, or you lie next to your husband after you've made love and breathe the heat of his merciless dreams and wonder who he is, tenderly ponder the truth you'll never know, because this is the secret that sleep protects in its neural depths, in its stages, layers and folds.

This morning she talked about his name, or tried

to. They did it together, start and stop. But the more they talked—they talked a while and changed the subject and he turned off the recorder and she turned it back on and maybe he'd had one, yes, a name, but he'd forgotten it or lost it and could not get it back.

She said, "I am Lauren."

She said this a number of times, pointing at herself, because she thought it would be helpful to both of them if he called her by her name.

She said, "If you had a name. Just suppose now. Is there anyone who would know what it is? Where is your mother? When I say mother, the woman who gives birth to a child, the parent, the female parent, does this word? Tell me. What?"

He knew what a chair is called and a window and a wall but not the tape recorder, although he knew how to turn it off, and not, it seemed, who his mother was or where she might be found.

"If there is another language you speak," she told him, "say some words."

"Say some words."

"Say some words. Doesn't matter if I can't understand."

"Say some words to say some words."

"All right. Be a Zen master, you little creep. How do you know what I said to my husband? Where were you? Were you here, somewhere, listening? My voice. It sounded word for word. Tell me about this."

When there was a pause in the conversation, the recorder stopped hissing. She watched him. She tried to press him on the matter but got nowhere and changed the subject again.

"What did you mean earlier yesterday when you said, when you seemed to say what? I don't recall the words exactly. It was yesterday. The day before today. You said I'd still be here, I think, when the lease. Do you remember this? When I'm supposed to leave. You said I do not."

"I said this what I said."

"You said this. That you somehow."

"Somehow. What is somehow?"

"Shut up. That you somehow but never mind. When the lease ends. Or something else completely."

He turned off the recorder. She turned it on, he turned it off. Just curious, she thought, or aimlessly playing. But she felt like hitting him. No, she didn't. She didn't know what she felt. It was time to call the hospitals and other institutions. That's what she felt. It was way past the time and she was making a mistake not to inquire, not to take him to someone in a position of authority, a doctor or administrator, the nun who runs an assisted-living shelter, gracious and able, but she knew she would not do it.

She spent an hour in a makeshift office on the second floor, transcribing selected remarks from the tape she'd made with him.

She heard herself say, "I am Lauren," like a character in black spandex in a science-fiction film.

It occurred to her finally. She began to understand that he'd heard her voice on the tape recorder. At some point before she'd inserted a blank tape, he'd hit the play button and heard her talking to Rey, who was up on the second floor with the tape machine in his hand, communicating script ideas.

That's how he reproduced her voice.

What about the hand gesture? She rejected the hand gesture. The gesture was coincidental, circumstantial, partly her own fabrication.

She felt better now.

Over the days she worked her body hard. There were always states to reach that surpassed previous extremes. She could take a thing to an unendurable extreme as measured by breath or strength or length of time or force of will and then resolve to extend the limit.

I think you are making your own little totalitarian

society, Rey told her once, where you are the dictator, absolutely, and also the oppressed people, he said, perhaps admiringly, one artist to another.

Her bodywork made everything transparent. She saw and thought clearly, which might only mean there was little that needed seeing and not a lot to think about. But maybe it went deeper, the poses she assumed and held for prolonged periods, the gyrate exaggerations, the snake shapes and flower bends, the prayerful spans of systematic breathing, life lived irreducibly as sheer respiration. First breathe, then pant, then gasp. It made her go taut and saucer-eyed, arteries flaring in her neck, these hours of breathing so urgent and absurd that she came out the other end in a kind of pristine light, feeling what it means to be alive.

She began to work naked in a cold room. She did her crossovers on the bare floor, and her pelvic stretches, which were mockingly erotic and erotic both, and her slow-motion repetitions of everyday gestures, checking the time on your wrist or turning to hail a cab, actions quoted by rote in another conceptual frame, many times over and now slower and over, with your mouth open in astonishment and your eyes shut tight against the intensity of passing awareness.

*

Isabel called, Rey's first wife.

"At the funeral we barely talked. So you avoided me a little, which I understand it, believe me, and can sympathize. I also accept what he did because I know him forever. But for you it's different. I feel bad we didn't talk. I could see it coming for years. This is a thing that was going to happen. We all knew this about him. For years he was going to do this thing. It was a thing he carried with him. It was his way out. He wasn't a man in despair. This thing was a plan in his mind. It was his trick that he knew he could do when he needed it. He even made me see him in the chair."

"But don't you understand?"

"Please. Who understands but me? He was an impossible man. From Paris already he was very difficult. Nearly eleven years we were married. I went through things with him I could not begin to tell you. Don't think I am not sparing you. I am sparing you everything. This man, it was not a question of chemicals in his brain. It was him who he was. Frankly you didn't have time to find out. Because I will tell you something. We were two people with one life and it was his life. I stayed with him until it ruined my health, which I am still paying the price. I had to leave in the middle of the night. Because why do you think? He threatened he would kill me.

And in this room where I'm standing I look at the empty space where the chair used to be. For one whole day it was here until they removed it out of my sight and took it to the medical examiner, with his blood and what else, I won't even describe, okay, for evidence. So I buy another chair. No problem. In the meantime there is the empty space. Of course he wanted to spare you the actual moment. So he comes to New York and sits in my chair."

"It was your chair. Was it your gun? Whose gun did he use?"

"Are you crazy my gun? This is another thing you didn't know. He always owned a gun. Wherever he lived he had a gun. This gun or that gun. I didn't keep count."

"No. Don't you understand? I don't want to hear this."

"But I want to say it. I insist to say it. This man hated who he was. Because how long do I know this man and how long do you know him? I never left. Did I ever leave? Were we ever really separated? I knew him in my sleep. And I know exactly how his mind was working. He said to himself two things. This is a woman I know forever. And maybe she will not mind the mess."

*

She went looking for Mr. Tuttle. She had no idea where he went or what he did when he was out of her sight. He made more sense to her sleeping than he did across the table, eyes slightly bulging, or in her imagination for that matter. It was hard for her to think him into being, even momentarily, in the shallowest sort of conjecture, a figure by a window in the dusty light.

She stood in the front hall and called, "Where are you?"

That night they sat in the panelled room and she read to him from a book about the human body. There were photographs of blood cells magnified many thousands of times and there was a section of text on the biology of childbirth and this is what she was reading to him, slowly, inserting comments of her own, and asking questions, and drinking tea, and about forty minutes into the session, reading a passage about the embryo, half an inch long, afloat in body fluid, she realized he was talking to her.

But it was Rey's voice she was hearing. The representation was close, the accent and dragged vowels, the intimate differences, the articulations produced in one vocal apparatus and not another, things she'd known in Rey's voice, and only Rey's, and she kept her head in the book, unable to look at him.

She tried to concentrate on strict listening. She told herself to listen. Her hand was still in the air, measuring the embryo for him, thumb and index finger setting the length.

She followed what he said, word for word, but had to search for the context. The speech rambled and spun. He was talking about cigarette brands, Players and Gitanes, I'd walk a mile for a Camel, and then she heard Rey's, the bell-clap report of Rey's laughter, clear and spaced, and this did not come from a tape recorder.

He was talking to her, not to a screenwriter in Rome or Los Angeles. It was Rey in his role of charming fatalist, reciting the history of his addiction to nicotine, and she heard her name along the way, the first time Mr. Tuttle had used it.

This was not some communication with the dead. It was Rey alive in the course of a talk he'd had with her, in this room, not long after they'd come here. She was sure of this, recalling how they'd gone upstairs and dropped into a night of tossing sensation, drifts of sex, confession and pale sleep, and it was confession as belief in each other, not unburdenings of guilt but avowals of belief, mostly his and stricken by need, and then drowsy sex again, two people passing through each other, easy and airy as sea spray, and how he'd told her that she was helping him recover his soul.

All this a white shine somewhere, an iceblink of memory, and then the words themselves, Rey's words, being spoken by the man in the chair nearby.

"I regain possession of myself through you. I think like myself now, not like the man I became. I eat and sleep like myself, bad, which is bad, but it's like myself when I was myself and not the other man."

She looked at him, a cartoon head and body, chinless, stick-figured, but he knew how to make her husband live in the air that rushed from his lungs into his vocal folds—air to sounds, sounds to words, words the man, shaped faithfully on his lips and tongue.

She whispered, "What are you doing?"

"I am doing. This yes that. Say some words."

"Did you ever? Look at me. Did you ever talk to Rey? The way we are talking now."

"We are talking now."

"Yes. Are you saying yes? Say yes. When did you know him?"

"I know him where he was."

"Then and now. Is that what you're saying? Did

you stand outside the room and hear us talking? When I say Rey, do you know who I mean? Talking in a room. He and I."

He let his body shift, briefly, side to side, a mechanical wag, a tick and a tock, like the first toy ever built with moving parts.

She didn't know how to think about this. There was something raw in the moment, open-wounded. It bared her to things that were outside her experience but desperately central, somehow, at the same time.

Somehow. What is somehow?

She asked him questions and he talked in his own voice, which was reedy and thin and trapped in tenses and inflections, in singsong conjugations, and she became aware that she was describing what he said to some third person in her mind, maybe her friend Mariella, objective, dependable, able to advise, known to be frank, even as she listened possessively to every word he spoke.

She began to carry the tape recorder everywhere she went. It was small and light and slipped into her breast pocket. She wore flannel shirts with flap pockets. She wore insulated boots and walked for hours along the edge of saltgrass marshes and down the middle of lost roads and she listened to Mr. Tuttle.

She looked at her face in the bathroom mirror and tried to understand why it looked different from the same face downstairs, in the full-length mirror in the front hall, although it shouldn't be hard to understand at all, she thought, because faces look different all the time and everywhere, based on a hundred daily variables, but then again, she thought, why do I look different?

She didn't take him into town because someone might know him there and because he never left the house by choice, to her knowledge, and she didn't want to force him into an experience that might frighten him, but mostly she wanted to keep him from being seen by others.

But then she took him with her to the sprawling malls, inland, in the thickness of car smog and nudging traffic, and she did it the way you do something even stranger than all the things you judged too strange to do, on impulse, to ease a need for rash gestures and faintly and vainly perhaps to see things through his eyes, the world in geometric form, patterned and stacked, and the long aisles of products and the shoppers in soft-shoe trance and whatever else might warrant his regard that you have forgotten how to see.

But when they got there she left him strapped in his seatbelt and locked in the car while she went to the electronics store and supermarket and shoe outlet. She bought him a pair of shoes and some socks. She bought blank tapes for the voice recorder, unavailable in town, and came back to the car with bags of groceries in a gleaming cart and found him sitting in piss and shit.

Maybe this man experiences another kind of reality where he is here and there, before and after, and he moves from one to the other shatteringly, in a state of collapse, minus an identity, a language, a way to enjoy the savor of the honey-coated toast she watches him eat.

She thought maybe he lived in a kind of time that had no narrative quality. What else did she think? She sat in the nearly bare office on the second floor and didn't know what else she thought.

They spoke every morning at the glass-top table on the sunporch and she recorded what they said. The room was unheated but they sat comfortably in the current run of sunny days over mugs of mint tea.

He sat hunched, speaking toward the device, sometimes into it, seemingly to it, with it, just he and it, and when he stopped cold, between constructions, his mouth continued to vibrate slightly, a shadow movement that resembled an old person's tremor of reflex or agitation.

"Did you know Rey? Do you know who I mean when I say Rey?"

"It is not able."

"Try to answer. Please. You see how important it is to me. Talk like him. Say some words."

There's a code in the simplest conversation that tells the speakers what's going on outside the bare acoustics. This was missing when they talked. There was a missing beat. It was hard for her to find the tempo. All they had were unadjusted words. She lost touch with him, lost interest sometimes, couldn't locate rhythmic intervals or time cues or even the mutters and hums, the audible pauses that pace a remark. He didn't register facial responses to things she said and this threw her off. There were no grades of emphasis here and flatness there. She began to understand that their talks had no time sense and that all the references at the unspoken level, the things a man speaking Dutch might share with a man speaking Chinese—all this was missing here.

"Push the thing."

"Push the button. No, do not push the button. That's the stop button. Did you hear us in the room? He and I. Talking."

She wanted to touch him. She'd never touched him, she didn't think, or did passingly, maybe, once, strapping him into his seat in the car, when he was wearing a sweater or jacket.

"You know him where he was. You know him from before. You heard him speak to me. Did we see you? Were you hidden somewhere so we could not see you? Understand hidden? You know his voice. Make me hear it."

She knew, she told herself she was not an unstrung woman who encounters a person responsive to psychic forces, able to put her in touch with her late husband.

This was something else.

She watched him. His hair looked chalky today. He seemed barely here, four feet away from her. He didn't know how to measure himself to what we call the Now. What is that anyway? It's possible there's no such thing for those who do not take it as a matter of faith. Maybe it was a physicist she needed to talk to, someone, she wasn't sure, who might tell her what the parameters were. She hated that word. She used it but didn't know what it meant and used it anyway. The birds were going crazy on the feeder.

She called Mariella and got the machine. A synthe-sized voice said, *Please / leave / a mess/age / af/ter / the / tone.* The words were not spoken but generated and they were separated by brief but deep dimen-sions. She hung up and called back, just to hear the voice again. How strange the discontinuity. It seemed a quantum hop, one word to the next. She hung up and called back. One voice for each word. Seven different voices. Not seven different voices but one male voice in seven time cycles. But not male exactly either. And not words so much as syllables but not that either. She hung up and called back.

She walked down the long hall and up the stairs to the third floor and past the empty rooms to the bathroom near the far end. He was sitting in the tub when she opened the door. He did not move his head or in any way acknowledge. She stood there looking. He had soap in one hand and a washcloth in the other. He remained in this position, hands poised, and she watched him. He did not move. He did not look at her or acknowledge by other means.

His hands were barely out of the water, the sliver of soap, the washcloth bunched. Soap is called a sliver in this figuration.

She whispered, "Look at me."

When he did this, unbashfully, she got on her knees at the side of the tub and took the washcloth out of his hand. She moved it side to side over his shoulders and down his back. She washed in the hollow under the arm. This is the armpit, one and two. She took the soap out of his other hand and rubbed it on the cloth and washed his chest and arms, wordlessly naming his parts for him. She set the cloth down gently on the water, where it plumed inward and sank, and she swabbed his belly under the water with the soap, a drone of motion, her hand slowly circling his navel. Then she leaned across him to place the soap in the soap dish, the sliver of soap, watching him all the time, and she put her hand in the water and eased along the penis, here it is, and cupped and rubbed the testicles, naming and numbering his parts, one and two, and a small moist glow showed above his lips.

His hand came out of the water holding the cloth. She took it from him and held it spread across her face and pressed into the pores and she rubbed it over her mouth and gave it back to him. She touched his face, which was lightly fuzzed, and does he shave and who taught him, and ran her finger softly across his mouth, tracing the shape of his lips. She traced his nose and brows and the rim of his ear and the swirled inner surface. This followed by that. This leading to that. He was not skittish under her touch, or only routinely so, and she thought that nothing could seem unusual to him, or startling, or stirring, measured against the fact, the blur, whatever it was—the breathless shock of his being here.

She felt something wispy at the edge of her mouth, half in half out, that could only be a hair. She plucked at it and brushed with her thumb, a strand of hair from the washcloth, and she couldn't feel it on her face anymore and she looked at him and looked at her hand and maybe it was just an itch.

Then she went back down the hall and of course it did not feel to her that she'd been washing a child but then it wasn't quite a man either but then, again, this was who he was, outside the easy sway of either/or, and she was still finding things to examine, and wondering aloud about his use of a washcloth, which seemed a high refinement, and defending herself for her actions, and analyzing her own response to the motion of her hand over his body as she walked for miles through the blueberry barrens, in blowing mist, jacket fastened and tape reels turning.

"How could you be living here without my knowing?"

"But you know. I am living."

He half hit himself on the cheek, a little joke perhaps.

"But before. I hear a noise and you are in a room upstairs. For how long were you here? Talk into the thing."

"Talk into the thing," he said in a voice that may have been an unintended imitation of hers.

She was in town, driving down a hilly street of frame houses, and saw a man sitting on his porch, ahead of her, through trees and shrubs, arms spread, a broad-faced blondish man, lounging. She felt in that small point in time, a flyspeck quarter second or so, that she saw him complete. His life flew open to her passing glance. A lazy and manipulative man, in real estate, in fairview condos by a mosquito lake. She knew him. She saw into him. He was there, divorced and drink-haunted, emotionally distant from his kids, his sons, two sons, in school blazers, in the barest blink.

A voice recited the news on the radio.

When the car moved past the house, in the pull of the full second, she understood that she was not looking at a seated man but at a paint can placed on a board that was balanced between two chairs. The white and yellow can was his face, the board was his arms and the mind and heart of the man were in the air somewhere, already lost in the voice of the news reader on the radio.

She called Mariella's number and got the machine. She listened to the recording and hung up and then called again and hung up. She called several times over the next day and a half and listened to the recorded voice and did not leave a message. When she called again and Mariella answered, she put down the phone, softly, and stood completely still.

She said, "Talk like him. I want you to do this for me. I know you are able to do it. Do it for me. Talk like him. Say something he said that you remember. Or say whatever comes into your head. That is better. Say whatever comes into your head, just so it is him. I will not ask you how you are able to do it. I only want to listen. Talk like him. Do like him. Speak in his voice. Do Rey. Make me hear him.

I am asking you nice. Be my friend. A trusted person, this is a friend. Do this for me."

They came flying in straight-up to the rungs, fighting for space at the feeding ports, pecking at others, wings humming and breasts burnt white in the sun, feed spilling from their beaks. They flew off and came back, semi-hovering, nine, ten, eleven birds, others fixed to the window screen, some in trees nearby, not singing exactly but what's the word, twitter or peep or squeak, and they attacked each other on the rungs or scrambling in midair, the color-changing birds, the name-saying birds, the birds that feed upside down.

At night she stood outside his room and watched him sleep. She stayed for an hour and then went on-line to look at the cars start to appear on the two-lane highway that entered and left Kotka, in Finland, watching until she was able to sleep herself, finally, with the arrival of nordic light.

5

It was another slow morning, foggy and still, and the phone was ringing. She stood nude in the workout room, bent left, eyes shut, checking the time on her wrist.

Or sat cross-legged, back straight, breathing dementedly. She blew through her nostrils and made echoey sounds in her throat, visualizing her body lifting and spinning, a rotation with every breath.

Or went about on all fours, knees hip-distance apart, rump up, feeling the cat-length in her pose, doing the shoulder roll.

She stood and swung slowly about, eternally checking the time, half her body wheeling with the arc of the left arm, the watch arm, or the body levered by the arm and the head cranking incrementally like the second hand on the missing watch, mouth open and eyes ever tight.

She heard a plane cross the sky and then the light blinked off and on, the sunlight, the sunray, an event she assembled through closed lids, and she knew the fog had finally lifted.

When it was too damp and cold on the sunporch, they talked in the panelled room and she took notes and recorded. He barely spoke some mornings but was willing on others and they sat near the fire she'd built and the house was dead around them.

"Being here has come to me. I am with the moment, I will leave the moment. Chair, table, wall, hall, all for the moment, in the moment. It has come to me. Here and near. From the moment I am gone, am left, am leaving. I will leave the moment from the moment."

She didn't know what to call this. She called it singing. He kept it going a while, ongoing, oncoming, and it was song, it was chant. She leaned into him. This was a level that demonstrated he was not closed to inspiration. She felt an easing in her body that drew her down out of laborious thought and into something nearly uncontrollable. She leaned into his voice, laughing. She wanted to chant with him, to fall in and out of time, or words, or things, whatever he was doing, but she only laughed instead.

"Coming and going I am leaving. I will go and

come. Leaving has come to me. We all, shall all, will all be left. Because I am here and where. And I will go or not or never. And I have seen what I will see. If I am where I will be. Because nothing comes between me."

She was laughing but he was not. It came out of him nonstop and it wasn't schizophrenic speech or the whoop of rippling bodies shocked by God. He sat pale and still. She watched him. It was pure chant, transparent, or was he saying something to her? She felt an elation that made it hard for her to listen carefully. Was he telling her what it is like to be him, to live in his body and mind? She tried to hear this but could not. The words ran on, sensuous and empty, and she wanted him to laugh with her, to follow her out of herself. This is the point, yes, this is the stir of true amazement. And some terror at the edge, or fear of believing, some displacement of self, but this is the point, this is the wedge into ecstasy, the old deep meaning of the word, your eyes rolling upward in your skull.

"What is the moment? You said the moment. Tell me what this means to you. Show me the moment."

He said, "Talk into the thing."

"What do you know? Who is Rey? Do you talk to him? Did you ever talk to him? Do you know who

I am talking about when I say Rey? I am Lauren. Who is Rey? A man. So tall. Look. So tall. This tall. And a mustache. A man with hair on his upper lip. Look at me, geek. How tall? This tall. A man with brushy hair on his upper lip. But then he shaved his mustache."

He shaved his mustache. She'd forgotten this until now.

She saw something out of the corner of her eye. She turned her head and nothing was there. The phone was ringing. She decided to find an optometrist because she thought she'd seen something a number of times, or once or twice, out of the corner of her right eye, or an ophthalmologist, but knew she wouldn't bother. The phone was ringing. She picked it up and waited for someone to speak.

It was time to sand her body. She used a pumice stone on the bottoms of her feet, working circular swipes, balls, heels, and then resoaped the foot and twisted it up into her hand again. She liked to hold a foot in a hand. She patiently razed the lone callus, stretching the task over days, lost in it, her body coiled in a wholeness of intent, the kind of solemn self-absorption that marks a line from childhood.

She had emery boards and files, many kinds of scissors, clippers and creams that activated the verbs of abridgment and excision. She studied her fingers and toes. There was a way in which she isolated a digit for sharp regard, using a magnifier and a square of dark cardboard, and there were hangnails flying and shreds and grains of dead skin and fragments of nail, scintillas, springing in the air.

It was good to be doing this again.

Maybe this man is defenseless against the truth of the world.

What truth? She thought, What truth?

Time is supposed to pass, she thought. But maybe he is living in another state. It is a kind of time that is simply and overwhelmingly there, laid out, unoccurring, and he lacks the inborn ability to reconceive this condition.

What ability?

There is nothing he can do to imagine time existing in reassuring sequence, passing, flowing, happening—the world happens, it has to, we feel it—with names and dates and distinctions.

His future is unnamed. It is simultaneous, somehow, with the present. Neither happens before or after the other and they are equally accessible, perhaps, if only in his mind.

The laws of nature permit things that in fact, in practice, she thought, never happen.

But could.

But could not.

But could. If only in his mind, she thought.

She ate dull light dinners, quickly, getting it over with. Sometimes he didn't appear and sometimes he appeared but didn't eat and once he was missing for six or seven hours and she went through the house and then down the driveway in the dark, shining a flashlight in the trees and calmly saying, "Where are you?"

She waited inside with a book in her hands, a prop, sitting and thinking, not thinking, any woman who knows the worst.

He came into the room then, edgingly, in his self-winding way, as if, as if. She watched him try to adapt his frame to a wing chair and allowed herself a certain measure of relief, a kind of body lightness that disengaged her dreamily from the stolid woman with the book.

She thought of a man showing up unexpectedly. Not the man who was here now. Another man. It was nothing, it was something that came into her mind while she ate her breakfast, a man appearing suddenly, as in a movie, and he is shot from below. Not shot but photographed. Not shot-shot but captured on motion-picture film, from below, so that he looms. It comes as a shock, the way it's done, a man at the door, lighted in such and such a way, menacingly, for effect, or encountered in the driveway when she gets out of her car, a large man, looming suddenly above her. It is the shock of the outside world, the blow, the stun of intrusion, and the moment is rendered in a way that's deeply threatening to two people who have been living reclusively, in self-involved circumstances. It turns out that he is the owner of the house, a large man, yes, for effect, old but fit, or not so old, and it turns out further that he is here to talk about Mr. Tuttle.

She saw herself in the scene, in the driveway, listening to the man. It was just a passing thing, a story she told herself, or screened, forgettably. The man explains to her that Mr. Tuttle, by whatever name, is a family member of the second cousin type, or he is the son, this is better, of a beloved sister, and he has spent much of his life in this house, with an undiagnosed condition, or brain-damaged, better, and being cared for part-time by a nurse hired by the man, the owner, who is a little tweedy, a little shabby but mostly sad, sort of family sad, and when the owner and his wife Alma resolved to live elsewhere, with the children grown and starting families of their own, they decided to rent this old lopsided pile, their memoried hearth and home, and eventually probably sell, and they put Mr. Tuttle, whose real name does not get used, into a facility for people suffering from one sort of condition or another, a hundred miles from here, states of being that are beyond the most reckless surmise, and it never occurred to the family, when they heard he was missing from the facility, that he might be capable of finding his way back to the house, until now. It has occurred to them now, and so here he is, the owner, inquiring.

She refrains, in her imagining, as does the owner, from using the lost dog analogy as it pertains to Mr. Tuttle, out of whatever scruple and so on, and that was how the thing ended, more or less, over breakfast, with the owner and the tenant in the driveway, looking vaguely at the house.

The name Alma came out of nowhere. It seemed completely believable. Everything seemed believable, even the lost dog return, and the thing about the scene is that it never reached the point of does she turn him in, does she give him up, but just ended, abruptly, like this.

*

She walked on the grounds, feeling what was here, all sky and light, the sound of hammering somewhere in one of the hutments off the dirt road, nearly half a mile off, tactful on the wind, and how the clarity of things can deepen your step, give you something to catch at and grip, and then the hammer stopped. She walked and thought. It was one of the birdless mornings. A stillness hung about the feeders, such emptiness, arresting in its depth.

Inside she noticed first thing that he was wearing the shoes she'd bought him, snug, laced, with cushioned soles, and she was pleased about this.

They sat in the panelled room with the tape device on a coffee table between them.

Who had taught him to tie his shoes?

He was staring at her. He seemed to be staring but probably wasn't. She didn't think his eye was able to search out and shape things. Not like normal anyway. The eye is supposed to shape and process and paint. It tells us a story we want to believe.

"Then when it comes to me."

"What?"

"A thing of the most. Days yes years."

"Do you know what that means? A day. A year. Or did you hear me use these words?"

"Say some words."

"Say some words."

"In when it comes."

"In when it comes. What?" she said.

"Leave into leaving."

"Who is leaving?"

"This is when you, yes, you said."

"What did I say?"

She realized she'd never called him by his name. She spoke his name only when she was alone, talking into the tape recorder. Because, of course, admit it—the name is cute and condescending.

He said, "Don't touch it," in a voice that wasn't quite his. "I'll clean it up later."

He fell into a silence after this. Yes, fell. Showing a downcast glance, a lowering of spirits if she read it right. She recited a nursery rhyme, in French. She tried to get him to repeat a line and he made an effort, touching and hopeless, and she found herself describing the scene, mentally, to someone who may have been Mariella, or not, as if he were a piece of found art and they needed, between them, to settle the question of his usability.

Afternoons, ever so fast, last light drained into the hills across the bay, into everything around her, trees and earth and the pressed leaves beneath her feet, umbered rust and gold, and once a skein of geese passed silently over her shoulder, flying down the world into their secret night.

She began to understand that she could not miss Rey, could not consider his absence, the loss of Rey, without thinking along the margins of Mr. Tuttle.

When she picked up the ringing phone, she waited for the caller to speak first and felt a small cruel satisfaction in the lull of puzzled molecules.

She took him outside on a clear night and traced a constellation with her finger. It was a while since she'd looked at the night sky and their breath showed smoky in the chill air. She drew him frontally near and put his hands in her jacket pockets and blew words in his face that she made him repeat.

He said, "The word for moonlight is moonlight."

This made her happy. It was logically complex and oddly moving and circularly beautiful and true —or maybe not so circular but straight as straight can be.

She had to find a name that she could call him to his face.

She found it interesting to think that he lived in overlapping realities.

Many things are interesting, fool, but nowhere near true.

She reminded herself she needed batteries for the tape recorder.

She liked to think. What did she like to think? She was having a dumb day and wanted to blame the fog.

Maybe he falls, he slides, if that is a useful word, from his experience of an objective world, the deepest description of space-time, where he does not feel a sense of future direction—he slides into her experience, everyone's, the standard sun-kissed chronology of events.

Am I the first human to abduct an alien?

The fog was somber and bronzed low-rolling toward the coast but then lost form on landfall, taking everything with it in amoebic murk.

If there is no sequential order except for what we engender to make us safe in the world, then maybe it is possible, what, to cross from one nameless state to another, except that it clearly isn't.

She reminded herself she needed batteries. She told herself remember.

It was the kind of day in which you forget words and drop things and wonder what it is you came into the room to get because you are standing here for a reason and you have to tell yourself it is just a question of sooner or later before you remember because you always remember once you are here.

The thing is communicated somehow.

She wax-stripped hair from her armpits and legs. It came ripping off in cold sizzles. She had an acid exfoliating cream, hard-core, prescribed, and after she stripped the hair she rubbed in the cream to remove wastepapery skin in flakes and scales and little rolling boluses that she liked to hold between her fingers and imagine, unmorbidly, as the cell death of something inside her.

She used a monkey-hair brush on her elbows and knees. She wanted it to hurt.

She didn't have to go to Tangier to buy loofahs and orange sticks. It was all in the malls, in the high aisles, and so were the facial brushes, razors and oatmeal scrubs. This was her work, to disappear from all her former venues of aspect and bearing and to become a blankness, a body slate erased of every past resemblance.

She had a fade cream she applied just about everywhere, to depigment herself. She cut off some, then more of the hair on her head. It was crude work that became nearly brutal when she bleached out the color. In the mirror she wanted to see someone who is classically unseen, the person you are trained to look through, bled of familiar effect, a spook in the night static of every public toilet.

She used astringents to remove soap residues, greases and chronic lurking dirt. There were plastic strips that she stuck on and peeled off, grubbing up numerous pluglike impurities from her follicles and pores.

A hidden system, interesting, these tallowy secretions, glandular events of the body cosmos, small festers and eruptions, impacted fats, oils, salt and sweat, and how nearly scholarly the pleasures of extraction.

She found the muscle rub she'd bought for Rey just before he left and she used it just to use it.

She stood looking at him, two bodies in a room. He seemed to recede under observation, inwardly withdraw, not in discomfort, she thought, but spontaneously, autonomically, guided by some law of his body's own devising. She put her hands on his shoulders and looked into his eyes. She thought, When did people start looking into each other's eyes? This is what she did, searchingly, standing in the kitchen with Mr. Tuttle.

Don't touch it. I'll clean it up later.

His eyes were gray but what did it matter. His eyes

were off-gray, they were mild and still and unanxious. She looked. She was always looking. She could not get enough. His eyes were gray gone sallow in this harsh light, slightly yellowish, and there were no stirrings of tremulous self.

She framed his face in her hands, looking into him straight-on. What did it mean, the first time a thinking creature looked deeply into another's eyes? Did it take a hundred thousand years before this happened or was it the first thing they did, transcendingly, the thing that made them higher, made them modern, the gaze that demonstrates we are lonely in our souls?

She said, "Why do I think I'm standing closer to you than you are to me?"

She wasn't trying to be funny. It was true, a paradox of the spectral sort. Then she tried to be funny, using sweet talk and pet names, but soon felt foolish and stopped.

He ate breakfast, or didn't, leaving most of it. Then he stood in the doorway between the kitchen and the long hall that led to the foyer. She sat at the table, waiting. He looked past her or through her and she almost knew what was coming.

He said, "But where are you going?"

He said, "Just a little while into town."

He said, "But there's nothing we need. And I'll get it if we need it. I know what to get. We need some what's-it-called. Scouring powder."

He said, "What?"

She knew almost at once, even before he spoke. She didn't know specifically but sensed and felt the change in him. The tea was smoking in her mug. She sat at the table and watched him and then she knew completely in the first electric exchange because the voice, the voices were not his.

"But we don't need it now this minute. I'll get it when I go. Ajax. That's the stuff. There's nothing to scour right now."

She listened and it was her. Who the hell else. These things she'd said.

"Ajax, son of Telamon, I think, if my Trojan War is still intact, and maybe we need a newspaper because the old one's pretty stale, and great brave warrior, and spear-thrower of mighty distances, and toilet cleanser too."

Do you recognize what you said weeks earlier, and yes, if it is recited back to you, and yes, if it is the last thing you said, among the last things, to someone you loved and would never see again. This is what she'd said to him before he got in the car and drove, if only she'd known, all the way to New York.

"Just for a drive. This is all. I'll take the Toyota," he said, he said, "if I ever find my keys."

This is what the man was saying in the doorway, looking small and weak, beat down by something. It did not seem an act of memory. It was Rey's voice all right, it was her husband's tonal soul, but she didn't think the man was remembering. It is happening now. This is what she thought. She watched him struggle in his utterance and thought it was happening, somehow, now, in his frame, in his fracted time, and he is only reporting, helplessly, what they say.

He said, "Take a walk why don't you. Great day. Leave the car, leave the keys."

He said, "They're in the car. Of course. The keys. Where else? This is it. How can I tell you? This is always it."

He stood in the doorway, blinking. Rey is alive now in this man's mind, in his mouth and body and cock. Her skin was electric. She saw herself, she sees herself crawling toward him. The image is there in front of her. She is crawling across the floor and it is nearly real to her. She feels something has separated, softly come unfixed, and she tries to pull him down to the floor with her, stop him, keep him here, or crawls up onto him or into him, dissolving, or only lies prone and sobs unstoppably, being watched by herself from above.

She could smell his liniment on her body, his muscle rub, and then he was all through talking.

6

You stand at the table shuffling papers and you drop
something. Only you don't know it. It takes a second
or two before you know it and even then you know
it only as a formless distortion of the teeming space
around your body. But once you know you've
dropped something, you hear it hit the floor, belat-
edly. The sound makes its way through an immense
web of distances. You hear the thing fall and know
what it is at the same time, more or less, and it's a
paperclip. You know this from the sound it makes
when it hits the floor and from the retrieved memory
of the drop itself, the thing falling from your hand
or slipping off the edge of the page to which it was
clipped. It slipped off the edge of the page. Now
that you know you dropped it, you remember how it
happened, or half remember, or sort of see it maybe,
or something else. The paperclip hits the floor with

an end-to-end bounce, faint and weightless, a sound for which there is no imitative word, the sound of a paperclip falling, but when you bend to pick it up, it isn't there.

That night she stood outside his room and listened to him whimper. The sound was a series of weak cries, half cries, dull and uniform, and it had a faint echo, a feedback, and carried a desolation that swept aside words, hers or anyone's.

She didn't know what it meant. Of course she knew. He had no protective surface. He was alone and unable to improvise, make himself up. She went to the bed and sat there, offering touches and calming sounds, softenings of the night.

He was scared. How simple and true. She tried to tend him, numb him to his fear. He was here in the howl of the world. This was the howling face, the stark, the not-as-if of things.

But how could she know this? She could not.

Maybe he was just deranged, unroutinely nuts. Not that it's ever routine. A nutcase who tries to live in other voices.

He lay curled in a thin blanket. She uncovered him and lay on top. You are supposed to offer solace. She kissed his face and neck and rubbed him warm.

She put her hand in his shorts and began to breathe with him, to lead him in little breathy moans. This is what you do when they are scared.

She thought she saw a bird. Out of the corner of her eye she saw something rise past the window, eerie and birdlike but maybe not a bird. She looked and it was a bird, its flight line perfectly vertical, its streaked brown body horizontal, wings calmly stroking, a sparrow, not wind-hovering but generating lift and then instantly gone.

She saw it mostly in retrospect because she didn't know what she was seeing at first and had to re-create the ghostly moment, write it like a line in a piece of fiction, and maybe it wasn't a sparrow at all but a smaller bird, gray and not brown and spotted and not streaked but not as small as a humming-bird, and how would she ever know for sure unless it happened again, and even then, she thought, and even then again.

It isn't true because it can't be true. Rey is not alive in this man's consciousness or in his palpable verb tense, his walking talking continuum.

Nice word. What does it mean?

She thought it meant a continuous thing, a

continuous whole, and the only way to distinguish one part from another, this from that, now from then, is by making arbitrary divisions.

This is exactly what he doesn't know how to do.

She was working her body, crouched on the cold floor, smelling herself.

But it can't be true that he drifts from one reality to another, independent of the logic of time. This is not possible. You are made out of time. This is the force that tells you who you are. Close your eyes and feel it. It is time that defines your existence.

But this is the point, that he laps and seeps, somehow, into other reaches of being, other time-lives, and this is an aspect of his bewilderment and pain.

Somehow. The weakest word in the language. And more or less. And maybe. Always maybe. She was always maybeing.

She knelt, body upright and rigid, legs at hip-distance, head back, arms back, pelvis pushed forward.

Let arms drop down.

Dangle right hand over right foot and then left over left.

Everything flows backward from the pelvis.

Place palms on soles, matching hands to feet.

Time is the only narrative that matters. It

stretches events and makes it possible for us to suffer and come out of it and see death happen and come out of it. But not for him. He is in another structure, another culture, where time is something like itself, sheer and bare, empty of shelter.

Hold position.

Everything flows from the pelvis backward to the chest and shoulders and arms, to the furious flung-back head.

Hold position, breathing normally, then abnormally.

Repeat.

The wind started blowing at noon and was still shaking the windows when she walked along the halls five hours later.

The phone was ringing.

In the kitchen he dropped a glass of water and she extended an arm, seeing the speckled wet begin to spread on the plank floor.

The shrill wind made her uneasy, turning her inward, worse in a way than obliterating snow or deposits of ice that bring down power lines.

She built a fire and then walked out of the room and up the stairs, listening to the walls take the wheezy strain.

In the kitchen she said, "Don't touch it."

The best things in this house were the plank floor in the kitchen and the oak balustrade on the staircase. Just saying the words. Thinking the words.

She said, "Don't touch it," and extended an arm, held out a hand to forestall any effort he might make to pick up the pieces. "I'll clean it up later."

There's something about the wind. It strips you of assurances, working into you, continuous, making you feel the hidden thinness of everything around you, all the solid stuff of a hundred undertakings—the barest makeshift flimsy.

She cleaned it up now. She didn't wait for later. There was something in the moment that she needed to keep.

She picked up the ringing phone and it was Rey's lawyer at the other end. Something about debts. He was in heavy debt. There were obligations and liabilities. He had debts cascading on other debts. This made her feel good. It was Rey all right. She felt a rush of affection even as the news made her think of her own dimming finances. It was the Rey she knew and not some other. She was sure he hadn't been aware of the situation or had considered it so integral to the condition of his life that knowing about it was just another form of not knowing about it. It occupied no more consciousness than a soft cough on a summer's day. There were loans out-standing, accounts in arrears and taxes long overdue. The man recited numbers in a voice that had a government patent. He pointed out the implica-tions, the sinister transits of spousal responsibility. She laughed gaily and wished him luck.

Then he stopped eating. She sat him down at the table and fed him by hand. She urged and teased. He took some food, then less. She tried force-feeding him but he rejected most of it passively, head averted, or took it in and let it dribble out, let it dangle or spew.

She began to eat less herself. She looked at him and didn't want to eat. He ate next to nothing for three days running and she ate little more. It was suitable in a way. It was what she hadn't thought of on her own.

She looked at him. Poor bastard. She watched him with all the intensity of the first moments and hours but there was something in her look that felt different now, a deathly devotion almost.

Sometimes she followed him through the house. She watched him sleep. Mornings on tape, the questions and answers, little lessons and memoriza-tions, all this faded into a daze of stray talk and then more or less agreed-upon silence. She fed him soup while he sat on the toilet once. The days were tone-less and droning.

Finally she got in the car and began to drive the back roads, the fire roads, all the places no one goes, and she left the car and walked through fields to the highest point, the knoll or slope, and scanned the area with her hands cupping her face, looking for Mr. Tuttle.

From a long way off what would he look like, walking the way he walked, narrowly, in curved space?

Like someone you could easily miss. Like some-one you technically see but don't quite register in the usual interpretive way.

Like a man anonymous to himself.

Like someone you see and then forget you see. Like that, instantly.

She hadn't been able to find binoculars in the house and what was the point anyway. He wasn't anywhere out here. But she scanned for hours from different sites, hands at her temples to block the glare.

How could such a surplus of vulnerability find itself alone in the world?

Because it is made that way. Because it is vulner-able. Because it is alone.

Or you see him upside down, the way the eye sees before the mind intervenes.

She drove back to the house and walked all through it, room to room, one more time. She thought she'd climb the stairs and walk along the hall and go up to the third floor and find him in the small bedroom off the large empty room at the far end of the hall, as she had the first time, sitting on the edge of the bed in his underwear.

But when he wasn't there she knew he wouldn't be, if that makes sense. A few strides before she reached the doorway she knew he wouldn't be and then he wasn't. She'd known it all along.

She was left to wander the halls, missing him. He was gone so completely there was nothing left, not a single clinging breath of presence, but even as the rooms went empty around her, she felt something in her body try to hold him here.

She began to call the institutions, mindful of the irony, and she listened to recorded voices and poked option buttons and sometimes spoke to someone in a made-up voice of middling concern.

She gave herself two days to do this. On the afternoon of the second day she spoke to a director of psychiatric services at a small hospital about an hour south and he told her that a man who roughly matched the general description she'd provided had been admitted, pending tests, the day before.

She did not press for details. She wanted to believe this was him, being cared for and fed, clean and safe and medicated—free, finally, not to suffer.

But why should it be him? He wasn't mental. Why did she think of calling mental hospitals in the first place, just after she'd discovered him? He didn't act crazy, only impaired in matters of articulation and comprehension. Why did she ever think there was something psychotic about him except in the sense that people who threaten our assumptions are always believed to be mad?

But then it could be him.

She had a thing she stuck in her mouth, an edged implement, smallish, plastic, and she pressed it to the back of her tongue and scraped whatever debris might be massed there, a slurry of food, mucus and bacteria.

This was not a defense against the natural works of the body. This was what she did.

She calculated all the plausible requirements. Then she exceeded them. She shattered their practicality. This is what had to be done. It was necessary to alter the visible form, all the way down to the tongue. She was suppressing something, closing off outlets to the self, all the way down to the scourings at the deep end of the tongue, concealed from human view. The mind willed it on the body.

It was necessary because she needed to do it. This is what made it necessary.

His future is not under construction. It is already there, susceptible to entry.

She had it on tape.

She did not want to believe this was the case. It was her future too. It is her future too.

She played the tape a dozen times.

It means your life and death are set in place, just waiting for you to keep the appointments.

She listened to him say, Don't touch it. I'll clean it up later.

It is the thing you know nothing about.

Then she said it herself, some days later. He'd been in there with her. It was her future, not his.

How much myth do we build into our experience of time?

Don't touch it, she said.

He'd known this was going to happen. These were the words she would say. He'd been in there with her.

I'll clean it up later.

She wanted to create her future, not enter a state already shaped to her outline.

Something is happening. It has happened. It will happen. This is what she believed. There is a story, a flow of consciousness and possibility. The future comes into being.

But not for him.

He hasn't learned the language. There has to be an imaginary point, a nonplace where language intersects with our perceptions of time and space, and he is a stranger at this crossing, without words or bearings.

But what did she know? Nothing. This is the rule of time. It is the thing you know nothing about.

She listened to him say it, on the tape, in a voice that was probably hers.

But she could have made it up, much of it. Not from scratch. But in retrospect, in memory.

But she had it on tape and it was him and he was saying it.

Then she said it herself but so what. So what if she said the same thing in the same words.

Means nothing. People saying the same thing.

She had him on tape, saying it, but she might easily have misremembered what she herself said when he dropped the water glass. Might have been different. Slightly, very, moderately different.

But so what if it's the same.

Past, present and future are not amenities of language. Time unfolds into the seams of being. It passes through you, making and shaping.

But not if you are him.

This is a man who remembers the future.

Don't touch it. I'll clean it up later.

But if you examine the matter methodically. Be smart, she thought, and analyze coldly. Break it down and scrutinize.

If you examine the matter methodically, you realize that he is a retarded man sadly gifted in certain specialized areas, such as memory retention and mimicry, a man who'd been concealed in a large house, listening.

Nothing else makes sense.

It is the thing no one understands. But it makes and shapes you. And in these nights since he'd left she sometimes sat with a book in her lap, eyes closed, and felt him living somewhere in the dark, and it is colder where he is, it is wintrier there, and she wanted to take him in, try to know him in the spaces where his chaos lurks, in all the soft-cornered rooms and unraveling verbs, the parts of speech where he is meant to locate his existence, and in the material place where Rey lives in him, alive again, word for word, touch for touch, and she opened and closed her eyes and thought in a blink the world had changed.

He violates the limits of the human.

For a while she stopped answering the phone, as she'd done intermittently since the first days back, and when she began to pick it up again, she used another voice.

Her eyes had to adjust to the night sky. She walked away from the house, out of the spill of electric light, and the sky grew deeper. She watched for a long time and it began to spread and melt and go deeper still, developing strata and magnitudes and light-years in numbers so unapproachable that someone had to invent idiot names to represent the arrays of ones and zeros and powers and dominations because only the bedtime language of childhood can save us from awe and shame.

At first the voice she used on the telephone was nobody's, a generic neutered human, but then she started using his. It was his voice, a dry piping sound, hollow-bodied, like a bird humming on her tongue.

BODY ART IN EXTREMIS:
SLOW, SPARE AND PAINFUL

We are sitting in the dim upper room of an Arab café in Cambridge, Massachusetts, and Lauren Hartke is eating a goat cheese salad, stabbingly, like she's mad at it.

Between bites she talks about the recent performance piece she created in a dungeon space at the Boston Center for the Arts.

She has transformed herself shockingly for this event and although the brief run is over, she continues to look—well, wasted.

She is not pale-skinned so much as colorless, bloodless and ageless. She is rawboned and slightly bug-eyed. Her hair looks terroristic. It is not trimmed but chopped and the natural chestnut luster is ash white now, with faint pink traces.

Can I use the word "albino" and eat lunch in this town again?

"It's vanity. That's all it is," she says. "But vanity is essential to an actor. It's an emptiness. This is where the word comes from. And this is what I work toward and build on."

Hartke, 36, was married to the film director Rey Robles when he committed suicide. Her father, Dr. Robert Hartke, is a classical scholar who is spending his retirement as a field volunteer on archaeological digs in the Aegean. Her late mother, Genevieve Last, was a harpist for the Milwaukee Symphony. She has an older brother, Todd, who is a China specialist in the State Department.

"I don't know if the piece went where I wanted it to go," she is saying. "Some of it is still inside my head, reshaping itself."

The piece, called *Body Time*, sneaked into town for three nights, unadvertised except by word of mouth, and drew eager audiences whose intensity did not always maintain itself for the duration of the show. Hartke clearly wanted her audience to feel time go by, viscerally, even painfully. This is what happened, causing walkouts among the less committed.

They missed the best stuff.

Hartke is a body artist who tries to shake off the body—hers anyway. There is the man who stands in an art gallery while a colleague fires bullets into his

110

arm. This is art. There is the lavishly tattooed man who has himself fitted with a crown of thorns. This is art. Hartke's work is not self-strutting or self-lacerating. She is acting, always in the process of becoming another or exploring some root identity. There is the woman who makes paintings with her vagina. This is art. There are the naked man and woman who charge into each other repeatedly at increasing speeds. This is art, sex and aggression. There is the man in women's bloody underwear who humps a mountain of hamburger meat. This is art, sex, aggression, cultural criticism and truth. There is the man who drives nails into his penis. This is just truth.

Hartke's piece begins with an ancient Japanese woman on a bare stage, gesturing in the stylized manner of Noh drama, and it ends seventy-five minutes later with a naked man, emaciated and aphasic, trying desperately to tell us something.

I saw two of the three performances and I have no idea how Hartke alters her body and voice. She will speak on the subject only in general terms.

"The body has never been my enemy," she says. "I've always felt smart in my body. I taught it to do things other bodies could not. It absorbs me in a disinterested way. I try to analyze and redesign."

(Personal disclosure. Hartke and I are former

college classmates who have stayed in pretty regular touch. We used to talk philosophy. I sat in on lectures. She was twisted enough to major in the subject until she dropped out of school to join a troupe of street performers in Seattle.)

Through much of the piece there is sound accompaniment, the anonymous robotic voice of a telephone answering machine delivering a standard announcement. This is played relentlessly and begins to weave itself into the visual texture of the performance.

The voice infiltrates the middle section in particular. Here is a woman in executive attire, carrying a briefcase, who checks the time on her wristwatch and tries to hail a taxi. She glides rather formally (perhaps inspired by the elderly Japanese) from one action to the other. She does this many times, countless times. Then she does it again, half-pirouetting in very slow motion. You may find yourself looking and listening in hypnotic fascination, feeling physically and mentally suspended, or you may cast a glance at your own watch and go slouching down the aisle and into the night.

Hartke says, "I know there are people who think the piece was too slow and repetitious, I guess, and uneventful. But it's probably too eventful. I put too much into it. It ought to be sparer, even slower

112

than it is, even longer than it is. It ought to be three fucking hours."

"Why not four? Why not seven?"

"Why not eight?" she says.

I ask her about the video that runs through the piece, projected onto the back wall. It simply shows a two-lane highway, with sparse traffic. A car goes one way, a car goes the other. There's a slot with a digital display that records the time.

"Something about past and future," she says. "What we can know and what we can't."

"But here we know them both."

"We know them both. We see them both," she says, and that's all she says.

I sit and wait. I nibble at my baba ghanouj. I look at Hartke. What *is* baba ghanouj?

"Maybe the idea is to think of time differently," she says after a while. "Stop time, or stretch it out, or open it up. Make a still life that's living, not painted. When time stops, so do we. We don't stop, we become stripped down, less self-assured. I don't know. In dreams or high fevers or doped up or depressed. Doesn't time slow down or seem to stop? What's left? Who's left?"

The last of her bodies, the naked man, is stripped of recognizable language and culture. He moves in a curious manner, as if in a dark room, only more slowly and gesturally. He wants to tell us something. His voice is audible, intermittently, on tape, and Hartke lip-syncs the words.

Have I ever looked at a figure on a stage and seen someone so alone?

His words amount to a monologue without a context. Verbs and pronouns scatter in the air and then something startling happens. The body jumps into another level. In a series of electro-convulsive motions, the body flails out of control, whipping and spinning appallingly. Hartke makes her body do things I've only seen in animated cartoons. It is a seizure that apparently flies the man out of one reality and into another.

The piece is ready to end.

I take a deep breath and ask the question I don't want to ask. It concerns Rey Robles, their brief marriage and the shock of his suicide.

She looks right through me. I persist, miserably, reminding her of the one time we spent together, the three of us, in Rome, when Rey showed up for dinner with a stray cat on his shoulder.

The memory enters her eyes and she sags a bit. I want to blame the recording device sitting on the table. It's an ergonomically smart four-inch-long, one-and-a-half-ounce, message-storing digital voice recorder, and this is the devil that makes me do it.

She looks into space.

"How simple it would be if I could say this is a piece that comes directly out of what happened to Rey. But I can't. Be nice if I could say this is the drama of men and women versus death. I want to say that but I can't. It's too small and secluded and complicated and I can't and I can't and I can't."

Then she does something that makes me freeze in my seat. She switches to another voice. It is his voice, the naked man's, spooky as a woodwind in your closet. Not taped but live. Not lip-sync'd but real. It is speaking to me and I search my friend's face but don't quite see her. I'm not sure what she's doing. I can almost believe she is equipped with male genitals, as in the piece, prosthetic of course, and maybe an Ace bandage in flesh-tone to bleep out her breasts, with a sprinkle of chest hair pasted on. Or she has trained her upper body to deflate and her lower body to sprout. Don't put it past her.

She says she is going to the restroom. When a waitress shows up with the check, it occurs to me that I can turn off the voice recorder now.

The power of the piece is Hartke's body. At times she makes femaleness so mysterious and strong that it encompasses both sexes and a number of nameless states. In the past she has inhabited the bodies of adolescents, pentecostal preachers, a one-hundred-

and-twenty-year-old woman sustained by yogurt and, most memorably, a pregnant man. Her art in this piece is obscure, slow, difficult and sometimes agonizing. But it is never the grand agony of stately images and sets. It is about you and me. What begins in solitary otherness becomes familiar and even personal. It is about who we are when we are not rehearsing who we are.

I sit and wait for Hartke but she doesn't come back.

Mariella Chapman

7

The dead squirrel you see in the driveway, dead and decapitated, turns out to be a strip of curled burlap, but you look at it, you walk past it, even so, with a mixed tinge of terror and pity.

Because it was lonely. Because smoke rolled out of the hollows in the wooded hills and the ferns were burnt brown by time. There was a sternness of judgment in the barrens, shades of flamed earth under darkish skies, and in the boulders sea-strewn at the edge of the pine woods, an old stony temper, a rigor of oath-taking and obduracy. And because he'd said what he'd said, that she would be here in the end.

She had a grubby sweater, a pullover, that she put on, accidentally, backward, and then she stood there deciding whether to take it off and put it on again or to feel the slight discomfort of the neck of the sweater riding too high on her own neck. It was a crewneck, a pullover. She felt the label scratchy at her throat. Not scratchy but something else and she slipped her index and middle fingers inside the neck, elbows thrust up and out, thinking into the blankness of her decision.

They said grim winter grim.

But she is here again, in the house, as he'd said she would be, beyond the limits of the lease agreement. Not that she recalls his exact words. But this is what she'd understood him to say, or his inexact words, or his clear or hazy meaning. She has extended the lease, in whatever words he'd used, and she knows she has taken this action to fulfill the truth of his remark, which probably invalidates whatever truth there may have been. It is not circumstance that has kept her here, or startled chance, but only the remark itself, which she barely recalls him making.

She threw off the sweater and hit her hand on the hanging lamp, which she always forgot was there, and then pulled the sweater down over her head, front side front, as they'd intended in Taiwan.

She knew it was five-thirty and looked at her watch. That's what it was.

When she could not remember what he looked

like, she leaned into a mirror and there he was, not really, only hintingly, barely at all, but there in a way, in a manner of thinking, in some mirrors more than others, more than rueful reproduction, depending on the hour and the light and the quality of the glass, the strategies of the glass, with its reversal of left and right, this room or that, because every image in every mirror is only virtual, even when you expect to see yourself.

She climbed the stairs, touching the top of the newel when she reached the landing. This was something she always did because she had to, feeling the oak grain, the carved spurs and ruts in the wood. The post was tapered to an acanthus pattern and was the best thing in the house, just about, along with the plank floor in the kitchen.

She looked at Kotka, after dinner, in Finland.

For five straight days she drove out to the point, the headland, because the standing gulls that look a little dumpy on stilt legs become in their flight the slant carriers of all this rockbound time, taking it out of geology, out of science and mind, and giving it soar and loft and body, bringing it into their flight muscles and blood-flow, into their sturdy hammering hearts, their metronomic hearts, and because she knew this was the day it would happen.

She listened to the sound the wax paper made,

advancing along the notched edge of the box when she tore the paper from the roll.

The radiators began to clang, a common occurrence now.

She sat down to eat the food on the plate and thought I'm not hungry. The phone was ringing. She thought in words sometimes, outright and fully formed. She wasn't sure when this began to happen, a day or a month ago, because it seemed to have been the case forever.

Maybe she believed she could deliver herself into his reality, working out the logistics of word and thought, which is how he'd seemed to make his way through a statement or a room.

Maybe there are times when we slide into another reality but can't remember it, can't concede the truth of it because this would be too devastating to absorb.

This is what would happen. She played it through to a certain point, mentally, in the rooms and halls, and then it stopped.

She walked down the fire road past the ramshackle house with the freshly painted white cross rising from the point of the A-frame and the SAVED sign out front.

She cleaned the bathroom, using the spray-gun bottle of disinfectant. Then she held the nozzle of the spray gun to her head, seeing herself as doing what anyone might do, alone, without special reference to the person's circumstances. It was the pine-scent bottle, the pistol-grip bottle of tile-and-grout cleaner, killer of mildew, and she held the nozzle, the muzzle to her head, finger pressed to the plastic trigger, with her tongue hanging out for effect.

This is what people do, she thought, alone in their lives.

She was happy in a way, in many ways, folded in hope, having the house to come back to after long mornings rambling in stands of jack pine and spruce, where she named bog plants for him, spelling out the words, or whole afternoons when she crouched on the massive granite slabs out at the point, the promontory, and watched the weather build and the plumes of booming surf shoot higher, because this is what would happen when she returned, running her hand over shags of sea moss and knowing she would mount the stairs, touching the top of the newel at the landing, and walk down the hall into his time.

The stories she told herself did not seem hers exactly. She was in them so heedlessly they seemed to come from a deeper source, whatever that might mean, a thing that was overtaking her. Where did they come from? They did not come from the newspaper. She hadn't read a paper in some time. She looked at a paper in town, at the general store, front page only, and it seemed to be another framework altogether, a slick hysteria of picture and ink, the world so fleetingly easy to love and hate, so reliable and forgettable in its recipes and wars and typographical errors.

When she walked out of the store, she saw the Japanese woman coming toward her, the white-haired woman, and she wore a padded jacket and had her hands concealed. Her hands were fisted up inside the sleeves of her jacket, for warmth, and she watched the woman, sleeves seemingly empty, and cursed herself for not having thought of this for the piece, because it was fantastic, no hands, it was everything she needed to know about the woman and would have been perfect for the piece, inexplicably missing hands, and she tortured herself with the mystery of a gesturing figure, half lit, no hands, and smiled falsely at the woman when she passed.

Why not sink into it? Let death bring you down. Give death its sway.

Why shouldn't the death of a person you love bring you into lurid ruin? You don't know how to love the ones you love until they disappear abruptly.

Then you understand how thinly distanced from their suffering, how sparing of self you often were, only rarely unguarded of heart, working your networks of give-and-take.

She held these ideas every way she was. Eyes, mind and body. She moved about the town's sloping streets unnoticed, holding these ideas, buying groceries and hardware and playing through these thoughts to a certain point, in the long hall, among the locks, tools and glassware.

Why shouldn't his death bring you into some total scandal of garment-rending grief? Why should you accommodate his death? Or surrender to it in thin-lipped tasteful bereavement? Why give him up if you can walk along the hall and find a way to place him within reach?

Sink lower, she thought. Let it bring you down. Go where it takes you.

Sometimes she thought in these motive forms, addressing someone who wasn't quite her, and other times in other ways. She thought in faces, there in the air, the little missing man's when she could recall it, just outside the bony sockets of her eyes.

I am Lauren. But less and less.

When she got out of the car, someone was there. She wasn't out of the car, she was still half in, beginning to unbend, and a figure loomed above her in the driveway.

She nearly fell back into the seat. It was a jolting moment. She looked up at him, a large man, middle-aged, talking to her.

When she rose to full height, she was able to glimpse his car, parked at the side of the house. She listened to him. She tried to listen to what he was saying and to read the situation, fix its limits accurately.

"Assure you I don't mean to intrude. Tried calling several times. No answer. I understand completely. You're here to get away from that."

"And you're here?"

She was angry now. The looming effect, the menace began to fade. The fear began to melt back into her body, into the bloodstream and nerve fibers, the ridges of her fingertips, and she shut the car door hard, she swung the door shut.

"To talk about the house," he said in a tone of some detachment. "It seems this is my house, still. My wife's and mine."

He stepped back and eased around to look at the house, bringing it materially into the dialogue—his house. Now that he'd looked, there could be no doubt.

"And there is something you want to discuss."

"Yes exactly," he said and seemed to burst into a kind of pinkness, pleased by her grasp of the moment.

There was a pause. The man had a slightly edgeworn air, a malaise perhaps shaped over many years.

She said, "Who invites who in?"

He put up his hands.

"Not necessary. Wouldn't think. No, no, absolutely."

Then he laughed at her remark. It hit him finally and he laughed, showing sepia teeth. She waited. She was getting interested in this. She began to feel she was fitting into something, becoming comfortable out here, in the driveway, with the owner of the house.

"Has it been satisfactory then?"

"Mostly, I think, yes."

"Because if there's anything."

"No, it's fine, I think. Rooms."

"Yes."

"Rooms and rooms."

It was cold. She wondered if it was supposed to be so cold.

"Yes," he said. "Been in the family. Let's see, forever. But the upkeep."

"I would imagine."

"The work, the attention. We have a history of large families, I'm afraid. The endless sort of, you know, repairing, repainting. Something always needs attending to."

She waited for him to mention Alma in this regard, his wife, and the fact that the children were grown and living elsewhere now.

"And what we were hoping in fact."

His body stretched, it strained upward and askant in a little epiphany of bright expectation. She saw him in this gesture as a man trying to unsnarl himself from a lifetime's shyness and constriction.

"Is that you wouldn't mind."

She listened, practically seeing the words, and liked him a bit more, and felt an easy alertness, a sense of being inside the moment.

"Yes."

"You see there's a chest of drawers. It's stored in a room somewhere upstairs. Wrapped, I think. Probably wrapped in that padded fabric they use. Maybe you've come across it. Because it was about to be moved, shipped, and then somehow, well, you know how these things don't always happen when they're supposed to. It's a delicate piece, in two parts, and fairly old."

This is not what he was supposed to say.

"One of the unused rooms on the top floor,

wrapped in quilts. And what we'd like to do," he said.

She noted the tracery of blood vessels in his face, a large man, yes, and getting on, getting old, his skin beginning to stretch, eyelines deepening, and he was supposed to say something about Mr. Tuttle, why he'd left and where he'd gone and whatever else there was to say about the man, to clear up, to explain and analyze.

"Is, if we sent someone to get it, perhaps you wouldn't mind the inconvenience. We've tried calling and the woman has called, the real estate person. It's an old family piece. We thought we'd like to have it refinished and placed in our bedroom, at home. We've talked about it for some time. Current home, of course. But what with one thing and another."

He was afraid to stop talking because she'd given no indication either way and seemed to be disengaging herself from the scene. He stepped back and executed another half turn and they stood there in the cold, the owner and the tenant in the driveway, looking vaguely at the house.

She tried to remember what he looked like and then forgot his name. But briefly. It was only brief and it wasn't his name. It was her name that she'd given him.

In the morning she heard the noise.

She knew it was seven-twenty, just about, and looked at the kitchen clock. That's what it was.

She understood at once that this was not the noise from the third floor. It was different, not so high in the structure of the house, less furtive than before.

She stepped slowly through the rooms, knowing it would happen like this, as chant, a man's chanted voice, his, and it paced her way up the stairs and measured the flex of her hand on the newel. Being here has come to me. Because it was lonely, the coast in this season, and because she had to touch the newel every time.

She moved past the landing and turned into the hall, feeling whatever she felt, exposed, open, something you could call unlayered maybe, if that means anything, and she was aware of the world in every step.

She knew how it would happen, driving the car past the NEW USED signs, with firewood stacked in every lean-to and shrouded in blue tarp outside garages and barns. She'd return to the house and mount the stairs, past U-HAUL and AUTO PARTS, and walk along the hall on the second floor, in chanted motion, fitting herself to a body in the process of becoming hers.

She could hear him in her chest and throat, speaking hypnotically, and she approached the door to her room, the bedroom, not so high in the structure of the house. The room upstairs had nothing in it but a dresser wrapped in moving men's quilts. His time was here, his measure or dimension or whatever labored phrase you thought to call it.

She was a thousand times a fool. She moved toward the door and was a fool this way and that but not in her room, driving past AUTO BODY and NEW USED, with firewood stacked in canvas and sailcloth, because that's where Rey was intact, in his real body, smoke in his hair and clothes.

She knew how it would happen, past the point of playing it through, because she refused to yield to the limits of belief.

Once she steps into the room, she will already have been there, now, at night, getting undressed. It is a question of fitting herself to the moment, throwing off a grubby sweater, her back to the bed. She stands barefoot, raising her arm out of the sweater and striking a hand on something above. She remembers the hanging lamp, totally wrong for the room, metal shade wobbling, and then turns and looks, knowing what she will see.

He sits on the edge of the bed in his underwear, lighting the last cigarette of the day.

Are you unable to imagine such a thing even when you see it?

Is the thing that's happening so far outside experience that you're forced to make excuses for it, or give it the petty credentials of some misperception?

Is reality too powerful for you?

Take the risk. Believe what you see and hear. It's the pulse of every secret intimation you've ever felt around the edges of your life.

They are two real bodies in a room. This is how she feels them, in the slivered heart of the half second it takes to edge around the doorpost, with hands that touch and rub and mouths that open slowly. His cock is rising in her slack pink fist. Their mouths are ajar for tongues, nipples, fingers, whatever projections of flesh, and for whispers of was and is, and their eyes come open into the soul of the other.

She stopped at the edge of the doorway, aware of the look on her face.

They will already have slept and wakened and gone down to breakfast, where they muddle through their separate routines, pouring the milk and shaking the juice, a blue jay watching from the feeder, and she sniffs the granules in the soya box. It is the simplest thing in the world when she goes out to his car and takes his car keys and hides them, hammers them, beats them, eats them, buries them in the bone soil on a strong bright day in late summer, after a roaring storm.

But before she stepped into the room, she could feel the look on her face. She knew this look, a frieze of false anticipation.

She stood a while, thinking into this. She stopped at room's edge, facing back into the hall, and felt the emptiness around her. That's when she rocked down to the floor, backed against the doorpost. She went twistingly down, slowly, almost thoughtfully, and opened her mouth, *oh*, in a moan that remained unsounded. She sat on the floor outside her room. Her face still wore a decorative band, a trace across the eyes of the prospect of wonders. It was a look that nearly floated free of her so she could puff her cheeks, childlike, and blow it away.

She thought she would not bother looking in there. It was pathetic to look. The room faced east and would be roiled in morning light, in webby sediment and streams of sunlit dust and in the word *motes*, which her mother liked to use.

Maybe it was all an erotic reverie. The whole thing was a city built for a dirty thought. She was a sexual hysteric, ha. Not that she believed it.

She sat there, thinking into the blankness of her

decision. Then she worked herself up along the doorpost, slowly, breathing completely, her back to the fluted wood, squat-rising, drawing out the act over an extended length of time. Her mother died when she was nine. It wasn't her fault. It had nothing to do with her.

The room was empty when she looked. No one was there. The light was so vibrant she could see the true colors of the walls and floor. She'd never seen the walls before. The bed was empty. She'd known it was empty all along but was only catching up. She looked at the sheet and blanket swirled on her side of the bed, which was the only side in use.

She walked into the room and went to the window. She opened it. She threw the window open. She didn't know why she did this. Then she knew. She wanted to feel the sea tang on her face and the flow of time in her body, to tell her who she was.

picador.com

blog
videos
interviews
extracts